D0105232

THIS BOOK BELONGS to:

CR   5/16

Kate the Great

Except When She's Not

Suzy Becker

CROWN
NEW YORK

The Real Mrs. Petty

This is a work of fiction. Names, characters, places, and incidents either
are the product of the author's imagination or are used fictitiously.
Any resemblance to actual art teachers, Girl Scout leaders, or other
persons, living or dead, events, or locales is entirely coincidental.

Copyright © 2014 by Suzy Becker

All rights reserved. Published in the United States by Crown Books for
Young Readers, an imprint of Random House Children's Books, a division
of Random House LLC, a Penguin Random House Company, New York.

Crown and the colophon are registered trademarks
of Random House LLC.

Visit us on the Web! randomhouse.com/kids

Educators and librarians, for a variety of teaching tools,
visit us at RHTeachersLibrarians.com

Library of Congress Cataloging-in-Publication Data
Becker, Suzy.
Kate the great except when she's not / Suzy Becker. —First edition.
p. cm. — (Kate the great)
Summary: Fifth-grader Kate faces a challenge when her mother asks her
to be especially nice to Nora, a classmate and fellow flute player who is
sometimes mean.
ISBN 978-0-385-38742-2 (trade) — ISBN 978-0-385-38743-9 (lib. bdg.) —
ISBN 978-0-385-38744-6 (ebook)
[1. Friendship—Fiction. 2. Schools—Fiction. 3. Family life—Fiction.]
I. Title.
PZ7.B3817174Kat 2014 [Fic]—dc23 2013046710

Printed in the United States of America
10 9 8 7 6 5 4 3 2 1
First Edition

For Aurora, of course.
And my BBFF Jane.

↖ BEST BERKELEY FRIEND FOREVER

KATE, NOT KATIE

My best friend, Brooke, and I have Mrs. Block for fifth grade, except we are trying to pretend we are not best friends so Mrs. Block will put us together when she does the new seating chart, which we hope is extremely soon. This one is obviously not working.

DAY 6: THE SEATING CHART

Brooke is making this ridiculous begging face right behind Mrs. Block, and I have to think of something extremely sad (besides sitting next to Peter Buttrick forever, like Pop-Tarts becoming extinct or losing my electronics privileges) so I won't laugh.

"Okay, kiddos, let's put away our writing journals and get ready to go to specials." This is Mrs. Block's first year teaching fifth grade—she used to teach third grade, which is why she calls us kiddos and asks easy questions like "There are two kinds of writing, fiction and _____." Or "Are you ready for recess?"

HINT ↗

Easy Question du Jour: "Today is an F day. Who can tell me what our special is?"

Specials:

A GYM
B HEALTH
C LIBRARY
D COMPUTER
E MUSIC
(F ART)

I raise my hand. Meanwhile, she gives the class a hint: "It is circled on the board." Pretty much everybody is laughing except for Mrs. Block. I stare at my desk very hard and pray that Mrs. Block will not ask me to explain what is so funny.

My prayer is answered. Mrs. Block turns to look at the board, and miracle of teacher miracles, she is actually smiling. "Well, I'll never have to ask *that* again! What were the chances?!"

"Seventeen percent," Eliza calls out. Eliza is a math genius.

"Seventeen percent is correct, Eliza!" Mrs. Block is still smiling as we line up to go to art.

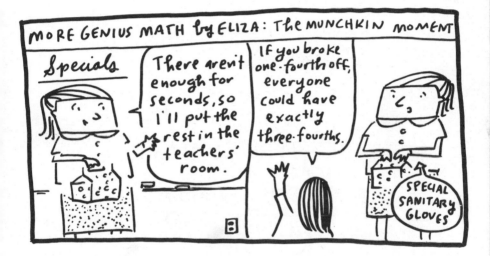

"Aren't you forgetting something?" Brooke asks, holding up her flute, which reminds me I am forgetting to make an announcement, so I raise my hand. "Mrs. Block, we do not need our instruments in band today."

Nora Klein is in Ms. Crowley-the-not-so-secret-girlfriend-of-Mr.-Bryant-the-band-teacher's class. Yesterday afternoon on the bus, Nora told me I didn't need my flute for the first practice, which is kind of unforgettable since Nora Klein is famous for sitting by herself on the bus and not talking to anybody.

THIS HALF·SEAT ~RESERVED FOR~ Nora's Personal Space

THIS HALF·SEAT ~RESERVED FOR~ Nora + Nora's Backpack

We wait while people put their instruments away, so we are approximately two minutes late for art class.

Mrs. Petty is at the door, looking at her watch because we are constantly running out of time for our art projects. News flash: NOT OUR FAULT!

"Mrs. Petty should time herself taking attendance," Brooke says. This is an extremely excellent idea, and my watch happens to have an excellent stopwatch.

Mrs. Petty

pet·ty 1. Small, trivial, or insignificant
2. Of narrow mind
3. Spiteful; mean

Reasons why Brooke is my Best Friend:

1. She has excellent ideas.
2. She does not act stupid in front of boys.
3. Sometimes she snorts when she laughs.
4. She has a corn snake and a TV in her room.
5. She has no younger siblings.

"Katie Geller?" Six minutes and twelve seconds later, Mrs. Petty is only on the Gs.

"Kate," I say. I have not been "Katie" since first grade.

"Kate," she repeats, and she makes a note for the fourth year in a row.

It takes Mrs. Petty fourteen minutes (13:49 to be exact) to finish attendance, which is more than a half minute per person, except she spends a full three minutes trying to pronounce "Hui Zong Tian," the new girl's name.

"It's *Hway* Zong!" I say without raising my hand. I will not let Mrs. Petty ruin Hui Zong's name. "Beautiful on the inside and smart on the outside, in Chinese." (We had to write essays about our names for Mrs. Block last week.) Mrs. Petty does not make a note of it.

KATHERINE: ← my best bubble letters

means "pure," which was news to my parents. They named me after my aunt and Katharine Hepburn (ye olde way of spellinge).

Twelve minutes left until band, *not* that I am particularly looking forward to band.

I am particularly looking forward to: a) getting out of art, *and* b) the end of band, which equals the end of the day, which equals Junior Guides, our first meeting of the year!!!

Q: How do you spell BORING?
A: B·A·N·D without instruments.
The ~~Old~~ ⁚NEW⁚ "HAND BOOK" → (one page folded)
1. Be on time.
2. Have your instrument.
3. Do your best.
4. No food, gum, or drinks.
5. Respect your fellow musicians, instruments, and music.

FARLEY
ELEMENTARY
BAND
♫

Mrs. Petty sits next to Brooke. "Today we are going to begin our self-portraits. Everybody please gather for a demonstration." She takes her piece of paper and sits it like a place mat in front of her. "I am going to do a self-portrait. Do I want my paper like this, hot dog–style?"

"No, I want my paper like this," she says, rotating her paper. "If I am going to draw myself, do I want a head this big?"

Zombie chorus: "NO."

"Like this?"

"NO."

"I want my head somewhere in the—"

Zombie chorus: "MID-dle."

PLEASE EXCUSE the INTERRUPTION: Students in the band are to report to Mr. Bryant's room. Students in the band to Mr. Bryant's room. Thank you.

The zombie trance is broken.

THANKS A LOT (not)

BEHOLD!
Music room door

BEHOLD!
Nora →
and
FLUTE

We run-walk to band. We are the last ones AND we are the only ones without our instruments. Mr. Bryant says, "You four can read along and turn the pages for your section-mates."

"Thanks a lot, Kate," Thomas Bergen growls on his way to the trumpet section. Meanwhile, I am making the world's pointiest dagger-eyes at Nora Klein, but she will only look at Mr. Bryant.

"Thanks a real lot, Nora." I turn and slide into the seat beside her.

gull·i·ble
Easily tricked

me

She has the nerve to say "So welcome!" Ugh, I could kick myself, and I am looking at my feet figuring out how that would work exactly when Nora Klein loud-whispers, "PAGE TURN!"

I reach to turn the page and my hand catches the bottom of the music stand and the whole thing wobbles but decides not to go over. Nora turns her own page in a huff, which she could have done in the first place, minus the huff.

Eight measures' rest—*oh yes!* Nora Klein cannot count her way out of a paper bag. She has to watch me sideways to see when I pick up my flute, but I do not have my flute and now *I* have taken up staring at Mr. Bryant. *Eight, two-three-four. Nine, two-three-four.*

TEN, TWO - THREE - FOUR . . .

Mr. Bryant taps his stand with his conductor stick. "Where are my flutes?!" I look at Nora. Problem is, I can feel Mr. Bryant looking at me. "Page turners, you have nothing to do but count. Cue your section-mates." He puts his stick down and sits on the stool. Here comes a speech. "Band, my friends, is a team sport."

Soccer and field hockey are TEAM SPORTS. Band is an option for people who cannot make SPORTS TEAMS.

"Everybody must give every job her best—refer to Band Handbook Rule Number Three!" (Mr. Bryant holds up three fingers.) "Not just for herself, but for the good of the team. Section leaders, those of you who have expressed an interest"—he is looking at me again—"are expected to be exactly that. Leaders." Mr. Bryant stands and raises his stick. "From the top."

Nora jabs me—"PAGE!"—and waits for me to turn the page back to the beginning, as if she didn't have any arms of her own.

I have a whole page and a half to figure out *how* I will cue my section-mate.

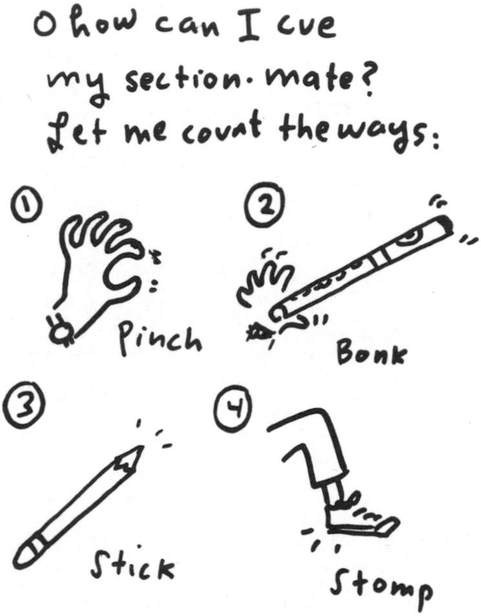

O how can I cue
my section-mate?
Let me count the ways:

① 🖐 Pinch

② 🎵 Bonk

③ ✏️ Stick

④ 👞 Stomp

In the end, I loud-whisper, "NOW!" Mr. Bryant shakes his head and keeps going. Here's something I never thought I'd say: I wish I were back in art class.

The page turners put away the music stands while everybody else puts away their instruments. "See you on the bus, Katie," Nora calls on her way out the door.

"Yes, please save me a seat!" I call back.

Brooke says, "Wait, you're not taking the bus!"

"Exactly! She was the one who told me we didn't *need* instruments. Besides, it's good practice. I've never seen Nora Klein save anyone a seat."

Brooke and I grab our backpacks and head to the cafetorium for Junior Guides. I try to put Nora out of my mind.

POD 429

This is my last year as a Junior Guide. I am pretty positively (not to brag) going to be a squad leader, and since I have zero intentions of going on to Senior Guides, I have a hundred intentions of making this the best year ever.

Mrs. Lawrence and Mrs. Hallberg are already in the cafetorium. So is Mrs. Staughton, Heather's mom. Mrs. Staughton is a substitute gym teacher. She's sticking around to help out. (You will never see my mother at a Junior Guide meeting; she is a lawyer and she works a thousand hours a week.)

Portrait of my MOTHER

*her regular "sec" = 20 minutes

Mrs. Lawrence is our leader. Now that her girls are in college, we are her girls. It's too soon to tell how long Mrs. Hallberg (the assistant leader) will last. Her daughter just moved up to Senior Guides and she specifically asked her mother not to follow her.

Helpy Hand

"Help your friends!

Other ways I can help Brooke:

No side conversations
No facial, throat, nasal expressions
Keep hands, feet, etc., to myself

"Do you have any jobs for us?" I ask. I am determined to help Brooke start this year off on a good note. Last year ended on a bad note, literally. She had to write Mrs. Hallberg an apology for calling her Mrs. Hurl Bag. (We all used to call her that, only Brooke got caught.)

Mrs. Hallberg said it was one of the loveliest notes she has ever received. I wish I had seen it because I personally cannot imagine how anything with the words "hurl bag" in it could be lovely. Anyhow, according to Mrs. H., "All is forgiven."

Mrs. Lawrence hands me the cupcakes so Brooke and I can put them out on a couple of Chinet $uper-premium paper plates. (We never get Chinet at our house.)

When you give a paperplate a piece of pie...

Me STRONG

me. TACO

Chinet   Ours

Unfortunately for the cupcakes (fortunately for us, YUM), most of the tops are stuck to the Tupperware lid.

Then I hear Brooke actually asking, "Mrs. Lawrence, do you have a knife so we can refrost the cupcakes?"

Mrs. Staughton has a Swiss Army knife. She also has two sets of plastic picnic silverware and twenty-seven thousand other things in her fanny pack. We refrost the cupcakes, and Mrs. S. watches her plastic picnic knives to make sure we don't lick them.

Mrs. Staughton

(and her fabulous, front·loading, foot·long fanny pack)

At 3:30, Mrs. Lawrence makes the quiet signal. Mrs. Hallberg raises her right hand high over her head and stares at Mrs. Staughton until Mrs. Staughton raises her hand, revealing a lima-bean-shaped pool of underarm sweat the size of Little Pond, our town beach. I am pretty sure everyone is noticing but I forget to ask them later, because what happens next is much too shocking.

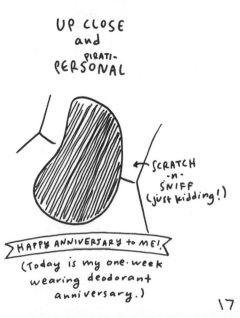

UP CLOSE
and
PIRATI-
PERSONAL

SCRATCH
-N-
SNIFF
(just kidding!)

HAPPY ANNIVERSARY to ME!
(Today is my one·week wearing deodorant anniversary.)

"Girls, I'd like to introduce the new leader of Pod 429—*your* new leader—Mrs. Staughton." Everybody claps because Mrs. Lawrence is clapping. Then Mrs. Lawrence says some words about finally retiring, but I have an ocean between my ears and I cannot possibly hear them.

what she says:

> after twenty-nine years, I decided it was finally time to give someone else a chance and

What I hear:

Next thing you know, Mrs. Lawrence is gone and Mrs. Staughton is ON. "Let's all stand and recite our Junior Guide Promise." You can still see a little of Little Pond with Mrs. Staughton's arm raised only halfway.

The JUNIOR GUIDE promise
I promise I will
not to cry right now
do my best to do my
BIG DOODY
duty to help all and
to respect myself,
others, and the earth.

"Can this day get any worse?" I say to Brooke, and she doesn't have to answer because Heather Staughton does.

squinty-eyes
Heather Staughton

"I HEARD THAT!" She squints her eyes at me and my stomach balls up.

I'm not saying that I could have, but explaining myself to Heather while her mother is talking and talking and talking does not seem like an excellent idea. "In conclusion, my main message to you girls that I have just taken fifty years to explain is this: We have some terrific things planned, but I am going to need everybody's help to make this the best year possible."

Brooke whispers in my ear, "*Translation:* I am clueless. Please take advantage of me."

"I HEARD THAT!" Heather says, all squinty again, except this time I know for a fact she could not possibly have heard a word. So, skip the apology.

I walk over all casual-like and say, "I was just telling Brooke I can't wait for your mother to be leader. It's going to be so much more . . ." I am trying to think of a truthful word.

"Exercise-ful," says Brooke.

Reasons why Brooke is my Best Friend:

6. She is talented at making stuff up under pressure.
7. She helps me out of AWKWARD situations.

Heather eats the frosting off a cupcake without removing the wrapper and puts it back on the plate. "I'm not so excited. Who wants to be the leader's daughter?"

I could see her point, but at the same time, I can see my mother jumping up and down outside the cafetorium windows and I have to make sure no one else does. "My mom's here, gottago!"

CRINGE·O·METER

"Is Heather's mom doing a gym patch, Monkey?" my mom asks on our way to the car.

"I wish." My mom moves the groceries off the backseat and points to my sister Fern, who is fast asleep in her car seat. "Mrs. Staughton is actually our new leader," I say softly. "AND she doesn't

believe in patches." My mom doesn't iron or sew, so that's probably the best news she's heard all day.

"I can't believe Shera Lawrence is moving on," my mom says. "What about your election?"

"We didn't vote. The 'jury's still out' on squad leaders AND the Big Spring Camp-In AND most of the rest of the best stuff."

"Well, let's just wait until the jury's back in." She puts my hair behind my ear. I put it where it was. "Change is exciting, Monkey," says the woman who thinks talking to each other is exciting, which is why we can't watch movies in the car.

Other THINGS my MOM THINKS ARE EXCITING

1. NPR
2. Scenery
3. Hiking
4. Gardening
5. Shoe shopping
6. Sitting by a fire
7. Brown rice!

Zz HELP! Please WAKE ME UP! I can't go on...

"Hey, guess who I saw at the supermarket?" She waits for me to buckle myself in.

"Abraham Lincoln."

interesting mole

"Great guess!" Mom smiles in the rearview mirror. "Mrs. Klein."

Honest Abe Lincoln
16th U.S. President
(as seen on penny)

AARGH... FLASH-BACK!

"Well, guess who told me we didn't need to bring our instruments today even though she knew we did and I got stuck turning her pages AND—"

"MA!" My four-year-old sister, Fern, is awake, which is a synonym for "end of conversation."

My sister FERN has **7** senses—
the usual five plus:

"!"   ","

6. She knows
when we're home
with her eyes CLOSED.

7. She only smiles
at nice people.

HE-E-E-RE'S ROCKY!

My mom and I do the bag brigade into the house. Two bags each, plus our own personal bags (my backpack, her briefcase), and my mom is carrying Fern. I personally think: a) Fern is too old to be carried, and b) my mom secretly hopes Fern will be a baby forever.

My dad is making dinner. Wednesday night is taco night. His hair smells like taco meat, technically turkey with the spice packet, when I hug him. "How was your day, Champ?" he asks.

"ROCKY!" I yell, which is *not* my answer. Rocky is our dog, and his head plus his two front legs are in the bag I just put down.

"Rocky, where's Fern? Go see Fern! Good boy, find Fern!"

PRESTO

OUT of the BAG-o!
Rocky loves all the food on
"Fern" Fern's face, etc.
Rocky!

ROSEBUD

"Nice one, Kate! I don't think I ever used you as dog bait!"

Meet my sister Robin.

Things I could say:

It is hard to argue—CORRECTION—WIN an argument with someone who is fifteen.

"How was Mrs. Lawrence?" Robin asks. "Did you say hi for me?"

"Mrs. Lawrence is retiring," I answer.

"Yes, it was a big surprise," my mom chimes in from the other side of the kitchen. "But Mrs. Staughton is going to make a wonderful leader!"

"Mrs. Staughton, the gym sub? Wait, what did we used to call her—?"

"Never mind!" my mother interrupts. "Kate, why don't you go feed Rocky?"

Translation: Kate, why don't you scoot, skedaddle, go on and run along?

Rocky has eaten the same thing:

$$2 \text{ times every day} \times 7 \text{ days every week} \times 52 \text{ weeks every year} \times 2 \text{ years}^+ \overset{!}{=} 1,456^+ \text{ times}$$

After I feed Rocky, I go up to my room. Technically it's
Fern's room, too, but Fern is never in it before dinner.

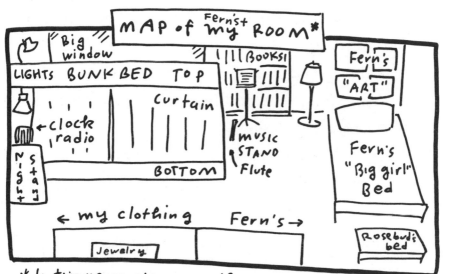

MAP of Fern's ~~my~~ ROOM*

"Big window" · LIGHTS · BUNK BED TOP · Curtain · ←clock radio · Night stand · BOTTOM · BOOKS · music STAND · Flute · Fern's "ART" · Fern's "Big girl" Bed

← my clothing · Fern's→ · Jewelry · Rosebud's bed

* In two years · eleven months · two weeks, it will be my room.

My flute is where I purposely left it this morning. I
take it out to practice. Rocky actually likes my band
tryout piece. His ears
won't tolerate anything
that goes above a high C;
Bach's Minuet in G never
goes above the G.

Johann Sebastian Bach

← Wig, duh.
(Real hair =
dark in color
style unknown)

Composer of Minuet in G
and 1,126 other things

27

"Dinner in fifteen!" my dad yells up.

Rocky and I go downstairs. "Sounding very good, Champ," my dad says. He is lighting the candles, which is normal at our house. We have candles every night, because according to Grammalolo, and according to my mother, who was raised by Grammalolo, candlelight makes children more peaceful at the dinner table.

BOB

I make two tacos and bring them over. Fern and I are identical taco twins—we like meat, cheese, lettuce, tomato, and olives. Lots of olives. No avocado.

I COULD EAT OLIVES on EVERYTHING!

yul. PEANUT BUTTER ✓

ICE CREAM ✓ Yes!

CEREAL X NO!

O.K., not everything.

Fern and I are the only ones sitting at the table, not counting Bob, who is technically sitting *on* the table between the two candles.

Bob is not filled with fruit or salad or decorations, like normal bowls. Bob is filled with so-called conversation starters. My dad begs everybody to

Meet my dad's brainchild

"Bob"

The Big Ol' Bowl

write down quotes or questions on little pieces of paper and put them in Bob.

BUILD - A - BOB!

1. Get a big bowl. Fill with "conversation starters." SAMPLE

OR

TAKE OURS! please! side door OPEN →

ADDRESS: 137 Pugh Road Kynlyn, PA

Everything has beauty but not everyone sees it. — Confucius

2. Pick a "starter" from your bowl.

Ancient Chinese Philosopher

3. Think about it for 24 hours (or more)

cracks make sidewalk look like brownie tops

It's kind of a miracle that grass grows out of them.

Really, everything?

4. 1) Figure out what you're going to say.
   2) Say it. (if the person who put the starter in is there, he goes first.)

was there litter in Confucius's times?

5. Repeat 2. Person who started conversation gets to pick. (you can put pictures in.) ⇒

Fern's Stink bug

"Okay, Ferno," my dad says once we run out of regular dinner-table conversation. He holds up Fern's stinkbug. "Bob's been waiting. . . ."

"Why are they so"—Bob has to hold on another half minute until Fern stops laughing enough to say— "stinky?"

Robin answers. "They don't think they're stinky. They make that smell when they're scared or they find a good place to spend the winter and that is how the rest of their friends and family find them. Their real name is brown marmorated stinkbug."

mar·mo·rat·ed
Marbled

Stinkbug

"Oh," Fern says. "Can bugs hear?" None of us know the answer. My dad writes the question down and tosses it into Bob.

My mom goes next. "Other than stinking, they're not bad as far as winter guests go—harmless in the house—but they've destroyed a lot of farmers' crops."

"They came over from Asia," I say before someone else does. "They've only been in the United States for fifteen years . . . same as Robin." I really hadn't been planning on saying the part about Robin; it came to me at the last minute. Both my parents laugh.

"Ha-stinkin'-ha," Robin says.

My dad goes next. "A place in New Jersey is collecting stinkbugs. They want you to mail it in a pill bottle so it won't get crushed."

Say thanks for CANDLES' magical peaceful powers

"You can mail a stinkbug?" I want to make sure I heard that correctly. My dad nods.

Dad passes Bob over to Fern. She closes her eyes and picks.

You must do the thing you think you cannot do.
      – Eleanor Roosevelt

Eleanor Roosevelt

← UNUSUAL

hat
...
smiling
in black
+ white
photo
...
5'11" tall

32nd U.S. President's wife
(F.D.R.)

SOME BIG NEWS

Fern doesn't open her eyes when I turn on my lamp. I am allowed to stay up and read until 9:15, which is what I am doing when my mom comes in and sits down on the edge of my bed. "Scooch over, Kate. We didn't get a chance to finish talking about Mrs. Klein."

"I'd rather not."

"When I saw Nora's mom, she had some big news— Mr. Klein has to go away on a long business trip."

"Maybe he can take Nora with him."

$\mathcal{E}_\omega =$

"Kate, that's not funny." *Translation:* That is funny, but it's not nice. "Mr. Klein is going to be working in Hong Kong until March. They're hoping he can come home over the holidays, but Mrs. Klein is very concerned about Nora. This could have had something to do with her behavior today." *Yesterday AND today.* "I volunteered—"

"Mom, *you* volunteered— you can't volunteer some- one else!"

me

vol·un·teer A person who offers HERSELF for service

"I didn't volunteer you. I suggested that Mrs. Klein sign Nora up for Junior Guides, and I said that I would talk with you. I think it calls for a little extra kindness—on the bus, in band, maybe introducing Nora to your friends at her first Guide meeting. That's all." *That's all?*

"Give it a chance." She kisses my forehead and turns out the light.

After my mom goes downstairs, I silent-walk to Robin's room. She looks up from her desk and waves me in.

Repeat after me, dear: We must do the thing that we think we cannot...

After I shut her door, we sit in our usual spots on the floor in between the two beds.

"Did Mom ask you to be extra-nice to Lexi?" I ask Robin. Lexi is Nora's older sister.

* OR under bed in case of EMERGENCY

"Mom didn't have to ask me to be extra-nice to Lexi. Everybody loves Lexi—well, everybody but Nora," Robin says. "But imagine being Nora *and* being Lexi's little sister. Lexi has a million friends. She's a really good student AND a total sports star. Then there's Nora. . . ."

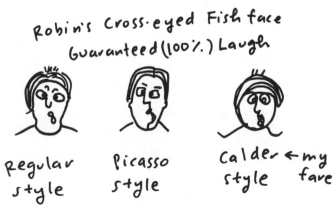

"Mom told me about Mr. Klein and Hong Kong. She probably didn't think it was such a big deal. You *like* being nice to people—haven't you earned a hundred of those school stars?" Robin asks.

"I don't like being nice to people who aren't nice to me." Robin doesn't say anything. "Besides, Mom wants me to 'introduce' Nora to my friends. You can't introduce someone everyone has known since kindergarten."

in·tro·duce To bring into use especially for the first time

"You must do the thing you think you cannot do," Robin says in a warbly voice.

"That's *not* funny." *Translation:* That *is* funny, but it's annoying.

"You *can* do this. You'll think of something. I have to finish my homework." Robin squeezes my shoulders and spins me toward the door. "Oh, I remembered what we used to call Mrs. Staughton—Mrs. Snotten."

"Thanks, but Heather Staughton's in our pod. And we don't need a repeat of the Hurl Bag Incident." I hug Robin good night.

N-O-N-O-R-A

Gene is the World's Best Bus Driver. 1) He plays our radio station. 2) He has a never-ending supply of mint gum in case you're bus-sick or just need a stick of something to cheer you up. 3) He does not give assigned seats (except to kindergartners).

I say hi to Gene—"Hi, Gene!" (get it, like *hygiene?*)—as usual when I get on the bus in the morning. Luckily Gene also has excellent hygiene.

```
note to self
~~~~~~~~~~~~~
BEFORE NAMING BABY:

#1. Say, "Hi, _____!"
                 NAME
   (Is that a word such as
      hygiene, hijack, etc.?)
#2. Double-check initials.

#3.  "  _  "  rhymes.
```

Then, as usual, I do not say hi to Nora, who is sitting in her self-assigned seat right behind the kindergartners on Gene's side of the bus.

> YOU must DO the THING YOU THINK YOU CANNOT DO.

> It's not that I can't say HI... The TIMING is all WRONG - not AFTER YESTERDAY anyway.

"Was she still saving you that seat?" Brooke asks when I get off the bus.

"Not funny." *Translation:* That is funny, but it's not helping.

I explained Nora's circumstances on the way into school.

"Extra kindness, extra-creative kindness . . . we can come up with something," Brooke says. She loves puzzles *and* she does not personally heartily dislike Nora Klein. (They are not on the same bus. They did not go to the same preschool. Their mothers did not make them have playdates.)

synonyms:
1. Not my favorite
2. Heartily dislike
3. Fairly despise

(Banned by Mrs. Block)

After five minutes in homeroom, we have come up with exactly zero creative kindness ideas. "Can we please think about my birthday party instead?" I ask.

"Slumber party, right? Friday or Saturday?"

"Saturday." My mom likes to collapse when she gets home from work on Fridays. "I get to have ten people since I am turning ten."

"Oh, that just gave me an extra-kind idea." Brooke writes something on the list and hands it to me.

GUEST LIST ☺
1. me
2. you
3. Eliza
4. Casey
5. Allie
6. Lily
7. Faith
8. Elsa
9. Bella
10. Heather?

10. ~~Heather?~~ <u>NORA!</u>

I shake my head. "N-O-N-O-R-A." When I go to erase "Nora," Brooke grabs the list.

"Wait!" Unfortunately, I have no choice; Brooke has the list and Mrs. Block has entered the room.

Mrs. Block rings her little bell. It's time for our morning meeting, the Share and Prepare part of our day. Peter Buttrick is sharing his Lego helicopter. In fifth grade, we are supposed to share ideas or current events, not Lego, but Peter's Lego is special.

Morning meeting ends early so Mrs. Block can have a word with Peter and dry off her desk. The rest of us have extra time for writing workshop, which

Thank you, helicopter.

R.I.Pieces

actually makes me appreciate Peter's helicopter. I ♥ writing workshop.

Brooke brings the guest list out at lunch. We update Eliza on the Nora Project.

"Do you think people would come if Nora—"

"I'd come," Eliza interrupts. "And I have no problem being nice to Nora for your birthday. Think about it. Nine out of ten guests, ninety percent, easily neutralize one out of ten, ten-percent Nora."

Except THINK ABOUT THIS:

ONE BAD APPLE
SPOILS
the WHOLE BUNCH

2nd PRIZE!
{I love making brackets.}
Scientific proof

{ ROBIN'S 8th GRADE SCIENCE FAIR PROJECT}

"But wouldn't Nora think it was weird if I all of a sudden invited her to my birthday party?"

"We have some time to figure that out," Brooke says, and she slides me three Goldfish even though sharing food is absolutely not allowed.

Being kind to Nora is going to be hard.

At least you don't have to start right away.

You have a plan!

Therefore I do not know why I did what I did on the bus except that we *did* have gym last thing and exercise is known to affect your brain.

INEXPLICABLE ME

ROOSE~~VELT~~ SHMELT

Everyone else in the family was very inspired by Eleanor Roosevelt's words, not counting Fern, who already thinks she *can* do a lot of things that she *should* not. My dad wrote two pages of his novel. My mother agreed to be the first woman on the board of the Dunleigh Hotel Corporation. *Translation:* She will be going to even more meetings. Robin and her friend Grace decided to run in the Gobble Wobble on Thanksgiving.

You go, Girls!

I might as well get it over with. "Sometimes *you* might be right and Eleanor Roosevelt might be wrong. Sometimes you *can't* do the thing you think you cannot do. Or you maybe shouldn't." I tell what happened with Nora.

Robin asks if I want to run with her and Grace, and I say no thank you. Running is not my favorite.

My mom pushes her plate toward the middle of the table and says, "That Nora is a challenge."

"Mmm," my dad agrees. "But it sounds like you gave it your best shot, Champ."

I lie awake after I've turned out my light. I didn't exactly give it my best-best shot, but I think "It sounds like you gave it your best shot, Champ" makes a nice ending for my Nora story.

GOODBYE, ROOSEVELTZILLA!

Unfortunately, my mom does not. She pats the bed in the dark and finds a place to sit down. "Thank you for trying today, Kate. I really hope you—"

"Mom, if you get to the fifth grade and you have no friends, there is probably a good reason why."

"Oh. What's the reason?"

"Nora doesn't want friends."

"It's possible. But it's also possible that she doesn't know *how* to have them. I just wanted to say, I know things didn't get off to a good start, but I hope you won't give up."

my PARTY INVITATIONS

Only kidding. I'm planning to send e-vites anyway.

NERVES CENTRAL

I would like this No-Electronics Soccer Tournament **[↗ Except mom]** Sunday to be over, but my systems are not cooperating. I cannot fall asleep. **[*I fairly despise soccer. Too much running, not enough GOALS.]**

STRATEGIES:

1. Counting backward from 100.
2. Relaxing my muscles from my toes-to-head.
3. Pretending I'm lying on the beach.
4. Putting my forehead on the cool wall.

The main reason: Band tryouts are tomorrow. I am half-excited and half-nervous. Half-excited, two-thirds nervous.

TRUE!! Everyone makes the band even if . . .

You still need help putting your instrument together.

OR You fall and impale yourself on your way to tryouts.

OR You hyperventilate and pass out partway through.

EMERGENCY → BROWN PAPER BAG

It's just that I want to make section leader so badly.

I give up on sleep and go to Robin's room.

"Why are you so nervous? Weren't you section leader at the end of last year?" Robin says. She shuts her door and takes *Human Biology* out of her backpack.

"That's why! No one expected me to be section leader last year. Now I *have* to be or else Nora Klein will be."

"Oh, I forgot about Nora." Robin reaches up to her nightstand. "Here, you can have Trolly for twenty-

four hours. He's gotten me through a lot of recitals."
Robin plays the piano.

ROBIN'S GOOD-LUCK TROLLY*
#rhymes with wholly and holy

He lost
his long
hair
in a
carsickness incident
before I was born.

We both hear someone coming up the stairs. I crouch lower. "You considering bedtime?" my dad says to Robin. "There must be something on the benefits of sleep in your book."

"Almost," Robin says, looking up from *Human Biology*. "Night, Dad."

I tiptoe back to my room. I sit Trolly on top of my flute case and get under the covers at 9:39. At 9:46, my dad turns on the TV in their bedroom, and the next time I look, it is 6:48, seven minutes until it's time to get up.

BEST
FALLING-ASLEEP
STRATEGY:

5. Listening to the baseball game and my dad snoring.

T.V.
zzz snores
sleep vapors
my
Bunks

my ROOM   my PARENTS'
                    ROOM

TROLLY MOLY

Mrs. Block is assigning "Colonial Buddies" for our new social studies project. I gasp when she announces that Allie and Ronan got Delaware. The gasp has nothing to do with Allie, Ronan, *or* Delaware. It has *everything* to do with Trolly, who is not currently in my pocket. He is lying, alone and helpless,

DON'T LOSE HIM!

↖ THE GHOST of the WORDS NEVER SAID

HELP! ROBIN! SOMEONE! COME GET ME!

on the reading chair in the Book Nook in the back of the library—that is, if no one has taken him.

"Excuse me, Mrs. Block?" I raise my hand.

"This will have to wait, Kate."

Hui Zong and I get Maryland, not Pennsylvania (everybody's #1 choice), and even though she's not Brooke (Brooke and Colin got Massachusetts), I'm happy that Hui Zong is my partner. I think she will do her fair share. After the thirteenth colony, Mrs. B. finally calls on me.

"May I go get something very important that I left at the library?"

"Sure, Kate."

Brooke looks at me with raised eyebrows.

A thousand phews. Trolly is exactly where I left him. This could be my lucky day.

MY MOMENT MUSICAL

"What did you forget at the library?" Brooke asks when we are finally on our way down to Mr. Bryant's room.

I show her Trolly. "Robin loaned him to me for good luck. Here..." I brush her cheek with what is left of Trolly's good-luck hair.

Reasons why Brooke is my Best Friend:
8. We are complementary.
9. She is complimentary.

your feet smell like flowers

"I hope you get section leader."

"Flutes first, again. Oboes last, again," Jacob Sweeney says. He has his reed in his mouth and is staring at the water, waiting for it to fountain. I would have felt sorry for him having to go last, but he was automatic section leader, if one oboe = section and being in charge of yourself = leadership.

TRY THIS at HOME!

Talking with a reed in your mouth is actually easy!

(Use half of a Q-tip.)

The schedule is on the whiteboard. It's alphabetical order, as usual: Elsa Adler is first, I am fourth, Brooke is fifth, and Nora Klein is sixth.

I put on my purple gloves, which people (not Brooke) may think is weird, but when my hands are a little sweaty, they play better.

DO NOT TRY THIS at HOME!

OR musically maybe
proven weird

NOT scientifically

period works for me PERIOD.

I do my whole warm-up routine, which I won't bore anybody with here,* but it keeps me busy right up until Anna Foley (#3) calls my name.

The KEY

"Keep busy!"

to NOT being NERVOUS

*CONGRATULATIONS. You're NOT just ANYBODY!

My WARM-UP ROUTINE

1. Play note as long as I can on headjoint.
2. Put flute together. (Do NOT listen to other people.)
3. Play C + G scales 3 times.
4. I told you it was boring.
5. Play Minuet in G.
6. DO NOT look at Nora K.
7. Repeat Steps 3-6.

I take three deep breaths before I open the door to the tryout room. Mr. Bryant's office smells like

SCRATCH
-n-
SNIFF ← I wish!

ros·in Resin from pine trees used to increase gliding friction on bows of stringed instruments

rosin and coffee and the peanut butter sandwich sitting on his desk.

From the time Mr. Bryant says, "Ready, Kate?" until he says, "Well done, Kate!"—after I finished the sight-reading piece "Moment Musical" (European for "musical moment")—it is exactly six minutes.

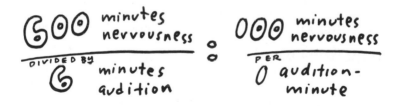

$$\frac{600 \text{ minutes nervousness}}{6 \text{ minutes audition}} \text{ DIVIDED BY} = \frac{000 \text{ minutes nervousness}}{0 \text{ audition-minute}} \text{ PER}$$

I stall in Mr. Bryant's doorway until Brooke gets there.

"Good luck," I say, and stuff Trolly in Brooke's back pocket. Then I point to the peanut butter sandwich. "Dare you!" She picks it up, and I swear, I think she's going to bite it, but she doesn't. I hope I didn't ruin her concentration.

Approximately seven minutes later, Brooke is calling Nora's name. She calls it a second time and a third. By then everyone in the whole band room is quiet. Except Nora, who is still practicing. I personally would have moved on to the next person, but Brooke goes and gets Nora, who acts more startled than grateful.

"I was hoping she'd wear the earmuffs during her tryout," I say.

"They kind of match your gloves," Brooke says, handing Trolly over.

"That's not funny." *Translation:* It would be funny if it weren't true.

When Robin gets home from hockey practice (another too much running, not enough goals sport), I give Trolly back. She says, "Trolly, you look worn out. Did you do a good job?"

ME?!
I was
ABANDONED!
An
ORPHAN-
left for
DEAD...

"I think he did. I mean, I think it went well," I say. "You don't think saying it went well is a jinx, do you?" Because I had already said it three times—to Brooke, to my dad, and now to Robin.

"Trolly offers expert jinx protection at no extra charge." Robin makes an X on my forehead with Trolly's hair. "I'm sure you did great, Kate."

CIRCLE ROUND the MOON =
SNOW or RAIN SOON...

It is a top-bunk night. The moon is coming up over the Wests' roof across the street. I stick Bob's quote on the wall.

The most important decision you will ever make is whether you live in a friendly or a hostile universe.
Albert Einstein

It's hard to argue with a genius, but I personally don't think you can go around deciding, unless you can change your mind. **ge·nius** A person of extraordinary intellect and talent Sometimes the universe is friendly; sometimes it's not. Nora Klein is proof.

I replay Mr. Bryant's three little four-letter words in my head.

Good night, moon.

CON ~~GRAT~~ BAD ULATIONS

My dad makes me pack my uneaten eggwich in my lunch bag. I get on the bus, say hi to Gene, and sit down two seats behind Nora.

LET'S NOT HAVE BREAKFAST for LUNCH!

Brooke is waiting for me in the bus circle. We watch Nora head to her locker, which is in the opposite direction of Mr. Bryant's bulletin board. "Hello?! Tryout results THIS way—could she possibly not care?" Brooke says. I am relieved because I don't want Nora knowing the results before I do.

Flute Section
Kate Geller*
Nora Klein*
Elsa Adler
Lauren Belt
Anna Foley
Brooke Johnson
*Co-leaders

Co-leaders?!

I am really glad I did *not* eat that fried egg sandwich because it would be coming right back out sunny-side up.

Brooke says, "I'd be happy if I was a section co-leader."

"With Nor—"

"With me. Congratulations, Kate." Nora is now standing behind us and I know I should say congratulations but all of a sudden my top lip weighs five hundred pounds and I cannot get it to budge.

VOL.

AWKWARD
SILENCE

"Congratulations, Nora," Brooke says. There are now at least six more people crowded around us and we are trapped until Brooke does this extremely loud, extremely real fake sneeze and the crowd parts.

Reasons why Brooke
is my Best Friend:

10. She can fake-sneeze.
11. She can fake-cry.

"It's just that whenever I don't think that I did well—"

"Which is most of the time," Brooke interrupts.

"I know, but this time I thought I did."

"And you were right. You're section leader."

"Section CO-leader," we both say.

"Jinx, you owe me a Pellegrino!" Brooke said.

"Morning, girls." Mrs. Block looks up from her desk, then looks back down. "Everything okay, Kate?"

"Me?"

"Kate made section co-leader," Brooke announces.

"Well, congratulations, Kate! That's wonderful."

"No, it—" And of all the stupid, embarrassing things, I start to cry. Mrs. Block stands up. "It's okay," I say. I have already stopped. "It's just that, never mind—no offense, but you wouldn't understand."

PELLEGRINO
Italian Soda

(Brooke doesn't like Coke.)

EMBARRASSING THINGS:

1. Crying.
2. Dropping lunch tray.
3. Wearing shirt inside out.
4. Farting during headstand test.
5. Farting during any test.

61

"Try me," Mrs. Block says, and she sits down on Peter's desk.

(Mrs. B. sits on Peter's desk.)

Now I want to laugh, plus I can see Brooke's shoulders shaking, but I don't want Mrs. B. to think I am having a meltdown. I try to imagine something extremely sad (besides sitting next to Peter Butt—forever) like . . . being Mrs. Petty's chair. "Last year I was section leader, not co-leader," I say, leaving the Nora part out.

"You two play the flute, right?" Mrs. B. says. "I used to play the flute. So did my sister. When I was in sixth grade, my fifth-grade sister was section leader. So I suppose you're right—I don't know what it's like to have to share the top spot, but I *do* know what it's like to feel disappointed." She slides off Peter's desk.

"Do I smell an egg sandwich?" Mrs. B. asks. "A little breakfast couldn't hurt."

In a way, the conversation with Mrs. Block helps, though probably not the way she hoped. Now Brooke and I know things nobody else knows about her. I would've offered her half my egg sandwich if it hadn't been flattened by my water bottle.

Brooke. Me. Mrs. B.

SPECIAL CONNECTION

flute   little   disappointment
           sister

MARYLAND TOP ~~X~~ ~~4~~ 3

"Congratulations, Kate!" Elsa Adler says from the doorway. I fake-smile and say thanks.

I have to do this about twenty more times, mostly at lunch. I am seriously considering making a sign.

After lunch, Mrs. Block hands out timelines. "Please use these to begin to organize your colony research."

Hui Zong and I have put together a page full of pictures of colonial Maryland facts and pictures.

I study it. "Tobacco, slaves, churches. Let's see—the governor with some Indians—"

"The Yaocomico"—she spelled the name for me—"Indians. They all died from the settlers' diseases."

"Maryland: Land of Smoking, Slaves, and Settlers' Diseases. Did I miss any good parts?"

"We have the Chesapeake Bay, and lots of rivers and water...."

The Birds and Wildlife of
Colonial MARYLAND

There *were* literally three interesting things about Maryland.

MARYLAND'S TOP 3 (or 9)

① 1-6* Baltimore is named after Lord Baltimore. *(There were actually 6 of them.)

Lord Baltimore

(as Voldemort)

② 7-8 maryland had its own tea party (possibly two) like Boston.

→ Annapolis 10/1774
"Legendary"
Chestertown 5/1774

③ 9 when the Continental Congress fled from the British in Philadelphia, they met in Baltimore (1776).

If you decide to believe, like Einstein said, that the universe is a friendly place, then Hui Zong and I are lucky Maryland is not the most interesting colony. For example, if there had been

EINSTEIN'S WORLD

twelve interesting things, we would never have finished early and had free choice time until the end of the day.

"Congratulations, Thomas," Mrs. Block says when Thomas Bergen hands in his Virginia timeline. Then she announces to the entire class, "We have TWO section leaders in 5B, Kate *and* Thomas!"

"TWO" section leaders?!

THROW ME in the STOCKS! (colonial punishment)

I make a beeline for Brooke's desk. "Congratulations, Thomas? I never even looked to see who the other section leaders are."

"I did," Brooke says. "They're all sixth graders except you, Nora, and Thomas."

BUSNESS AS USUAL...

THE NEWS
EW! EW!
EW! EW!

"Gimme five!" my dad yells downstairs. He means five minutes; he is still working in his office.

"I'll give you five hundred!" I yell up. I'm not really looking forward to telling him. I know it isn't bad news—Mrs. Block, or Brooke, or a lot of other people would've been happy to be co-leader. I'm not and that actually makes *me* look bad.

(I heartily dislike drawing circles.)

Rocky gives me his usual greeting. He doesn't care about tryouts or Einstein. He has way more important things to think about.

Any LUNCH left in that backpack?

"Well?" my dad says after he hugs me. He is standing with his legs apart like a short capital A so he can read my expression.

"Co-leader," I say.

"That's GREAT, Kate!" he says. "No, wait, that's not great; it's, it's—let me see, who's the other co-leader?" He is still reading my face. "Give me one guess." I give him half of an eye roll. "Nora Klein!" I nod. "Ah! I won the Grand Prize!"

phone case

GRAND PRIZE!

ANY ITEM from my DUCT TAPE KATE-A-LOG!

bow tie

wallet

shoes

pencil can

flag

belt

shorts

hat

← babysitter (just kidding!)

"Dad, I am getting used to the idea. I just wish you would tell Robin and Mom. It's not the best news."

"Roger that," my dad says. "I'll make a sign—naah, too best news-ish. I'll write a note and tape it to the door so Mom and Robin will see it on their way in."

I go up to my room to change, and then I check the note on my way into the garage.

ATTENTION
All ye who enter here:

Kate made section
co-leader.
Nora is the other co-.
I think it's great. You
may think it's great. Kate
is getting used to the idea.

Love ye,
Dad

"Thanks, Dad. I'm going to ride around Oak Hill. I'll—" And we both say, "Be back by five-thirty!"

"Jinx! I believe you now also owe me a Coke!" he says, pressing the garage door opener.

I ride my bike down three driveways and cross the street into Oak Hill. It's an excellent place for biking. No cars, three cul-de-sacs, and six side streets so far. The real hill they named Oak Hill after is pretty steep; it's actually nice to have something to mull over as you ride up it.

mole in

mull·ing
Giving serious thought

mulling cap

TRUE !! A steep hill is good for mulling and vice versa.

PEDALING

takes mind off

takes mind off

MULLING

I ride around the circle at the top, and then I ride down all the side streets, which are also named after trees. Still mulling.

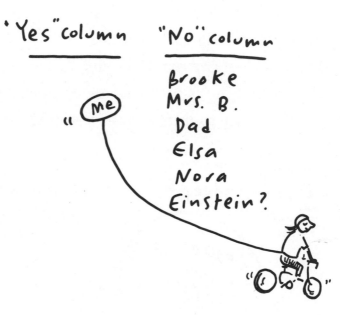

IS BEING CO-LEADER a DISAPPOINTMENT?

"Yes" column   "No" column

"me"   Brooke
                Mrs. B.
                Dad
                Elsa
                Nora
                Einstein?

"?"

By the time I ride down Hickory, I am mulling over what's for dinner. I look at my watch: 5:29! and race home.

EUREKA!

"Sorry about Nora," Robin says when I walk in.

"Well, I think it's wonderful," my mom says. "The wonderful part." She lifts my chin, and I can see from her eyes that she really means it.

"Are we having pie?" Fern asks, hugging my waist.

FERN'S & MY FAVORITE Lemon Meringue Pie

ALL-PURPOSE CELEBRATION DESSERT

"Robin made brownies, Fern," my dad says.

Fern lets go of me and runs to hug Robin.

My dad waits until the table is cleared and everybody has a brownie sitting on the plate in front of them, then he looks at my mom and says, "Einshtein?" Apparently she is the genius behind the Einstein quote.

Mom says, "Neither your dad nor I are scientists, but we both love Einstein," which explains the bike poster in the bathroom.

"Einstein was a brilliant philosopher, in addition to being a scientist. And when Robin was in my belly, your dad and I agreed that helping you look at the universe as a friendly, not-hostile place—this was how we were going to raise you. *And* Kate—"

"And me." Fern smiles.

GELLER FAMILY F★VORITE:

BROWNIE-PASTE SMILE

"Yes, we're doing such a beautiful job with you." My mom holds her napkin in front of Fern's face.

Other THINGS my mom THINKS ARE ⟨IMPORTANT⟩

1. Washing your hands before you eat.
2. Thank-you notes. (yes, NOTES)
3. Having dinner together.
4. Laughing.
5. Good night's sleep.

I guess it's good to know their thinking, kind of like knowing what is going to be on a test before you take it. Otherwise I might've wondered whether putting my napkin on my lap and being kind were the most important decisions I'd ever make.

"Robin?" my dad said.

"I'll go," I said. "Mine isn't really about Einstein or the universe. It's about the decision. People congratulated me all day long. I know a lot of people would be happy to be co-leader, but I was still disappointed. Until I was riding my bike and I decided I'm over it. But I still have to deal with Nora."

Dad says, "It's not always easy living in a friendly universe."

"Congratulations!" Robin says. At first I thought she was talking to me, but she is looking right at my mom. "Fern is the friendliest kid on the planet, and Kate and I both believe in the universe."

It was like someone had suddenly turned her into a grown-up.

"Well," my dad says. You can tell he is feeling proud of himself, and my mother, and the rest of us. "I have nothing more to say . . . except pass the brownies."

SAY WHAT?

Circle the BEST WAY to BEGIN your DAY:

GOOD
SONG
on RADIO-
ALARM

HEALTHY
BREAKFAST

NO NORA
on BUS

Therefore it is kind of shocking to see Nora Klein at band, but at least I haven't wasted the rest of the day dreading it. I am sitting there next to her putting my flute together and I think I hear her say, "I'm sorry."

So I say, "What?"

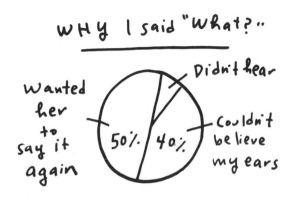

WHY I said "What?"

Wanted
her
to
say it
again

Didn't hear

Couldn't
believe
my ears

50% / 40%

"I'm sorry."

"Sorry?" I can think of a million—okay, exaggeration—at least ten reasons why she should be sorry, but I want to know hers.

"Sorry I made co-leader. I didn't deserve it. You're way better than I am." She hesitates. "Did you really mess up or something?"

MOM: "It's possible she doesn't know how to have friends."

So much for Nora's apology, but I am looking right at her and I can tell she's just curious. "Nope, I did pretty well. . . ."

Just then, Mr. Bryant raises his music stand. "Congratulations to all of you for choosing band and enriching your school experience. And congratulations to my section leaders. AND CO-LEADERS I see that everybody has music, stands, instruments. Let's begin!"

"How was band, Kate?" Mrs. Block asks when we are lined up at the end of the day.

I feel my face get red as I say "Good." I'm not sure if it *was* good or just a hundred times better than I thought it would be.

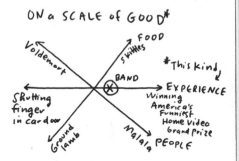

Or maybe it was good compared with what is coming next: "introducing" Nora at Junior Guides. I remind Brooke that Nora is joining Pod 429 on our way to the cafetorium. "Since when does she do Junior Guides?" Brooke says.

"Since her mom signed her up. Probably the night my mom saw her at the supermarket."

"Look." Brooke elbows me as we walk in. Nora is sitting in the far corner reading. Allie and Faith are helping Mrs. Hallberg with the snacks.

And then out of nowhere, Mrs. Staughton comes barreling toward us like a runaway train.

"The traffic was deplorable!" she complains, dropping her load on the cafetorium table for a grand total of fifty more exclamation points. "I'll be with you in four minutes."

"You have to say something about Nora." Brooke nudges me. I am just about to get up anyway.

"Excuse me, um, Mrs. Staughton?" She doesn't look up from her piles. "I was wondering—"

"I will be very eager to know what you were wondering once I am finished getting myself organized, Kate."

"It's just that Nora—"

"Nora, good heavens, I forgot Nora!" She snaps out of pile-organization mode and into fetch-Nora mode.

su·per·la·tive Superior to all others

Today's sweatstain

Factors- traffic, lateness, bright green suit.

"Girls"—she has her left arm around Nora and her right arm raised for quiet—"I want everybody to give a warm Pod 429 welcome to Nora Klein, our newest member."

"Heavens, I thought we were Junior Guides, not cheerleaders!" Mrs. Staughton looks uncomfortable. "Well, you girls have so much to teach me." Mrs. Hallberg offers Nora her seat, and Nora escapes from Mrs. Staughton's underarm to take it.

"I have a couple of announcements. After much careful thought and deliberation, I have decided we're going to have rotating presidents instead of squad leaders this year. I know this comes as a disappointment to some of you . . .

my HEART
↓
THUD.

"Heather will be our first guinea pig president."

Heather does not look super-excited. "The president will lead us in the promise and perform the other duties formerly assigned to the squad leader, and naturally, this will continue to evolve with your help." Mrs. S. unveils a monthly president chart.

PRESIDENT of the MONTH	
Heather	September
Brooke	October
Allie	November
Eliza	December
Elsa	January
Kate	February
Lily	March
Faith	April

February, as in the shortest month of the year before you take away the vacation?! "Mrs. S., you can give February to Nora, and I'll take May."

"Kate, I specifically gave you February because it is the month of our father-daughter dance, a very big responsibility."

For some reason, maybe having the words "responsibility" and "father-daughter dance" so close together, I think of Nora. "Nora's father will still be in Hong Kong," I whisper to Brooke.

"I'm sure she doesn't do dances." Brooke is right.

NORA DOES NOT DO:
- ☑ BIRTHDAY PARTIES
- ☑ DANCES
- ☑ ANYTHING FUN

Mrs. Staughton's idea of a Junior Guide craft project is making calendars where we can write in all of our meetings, the Big Spring Camp-In, school vacation days, everybody's birthdays, holidays, etc. We have just barely started when it is time to put everything away so Heather can be president.

PRESIDENT HEATHER

PRESIDENTIAL CLIPBOARD

PRESIDENTIAL POINTER FINGER

BOSSY PANTS

"We have to pick a Saturday for our Fall Fun Day," Heather orders. "The first weekend is out; I'm going to New York. And the second weekend is Columbus Day. That leaves the third and fourth weekends. Let's have a vote."

NOT the 4th WEEKEND

Special B-RAY GUN

Allie raises her hand. "The third weekend is my grandmother's seventy-fifth birthday."

Brooke is staring at me and I really, really want to say I'm having my birthday party on the fourth Saturday, but I can't since not all of the voters will be invited.

President Heather says, "Then it's decided. Mark your calendars. The fourth Saturday."

"But—but—" I stammer. "That's practically Halloween."

"Everyone can come in costume," Mrs. H. chirps. "Now let's join hands for the closing circle."

"Pardon me, Mrs. Hallberg," Mrs. S. interrupts. "I thought we'd try something a little different this afternoon. Let's close our eyes and reflect on our promise for a minute."

my PERSONAL
REFLECTIONS:

1. How can Mrs. S. reflect if she is counting?

2. How will Mrs. S. know when a minute is up if she is not counting?

3. A minute with your eyes closed is 25 times longer than a minute with your eyes open.

Something on Mrs. Staughton starts beeping and we get to open our eyes. "I would like each of you to share one thing you will do in the coming week to uphold your promise. Heather, why don't you get us started?"

There have been times I wished I was Heather, but this is not one of them. Heather doesn't seem to mind; she must be used to being a guinea pig. "I am helping everybody right now by going first." I have to admit that was pretty funny, but nobody is smiling.

"Thank you," her mother says, and she says it exactly the same way four more times before it is my turn.

"I will feed Rocky every day without having to be asked."

"Thank you."

Brooke says she will remember to turn out the lights when she leaves the room. And then it is Nora's turn. "Pass."

"Hmm?"

"Pass," Nora repeats, looking right at Mrs. Staughton this time.

"Oh no. No passing," Mrs. Staughton says. Nora just keeps looking. "It doesn't have to be something big; it can be something small. Anything, anything at all." Mrs. Staughton is making it into something big.

Nora is looking down now, and I think I see a tear fall out of her left eye. Personal weakness: I cannot stand to see anyone (except Fern sometimes) cry. "Mrs. Staughton," I say, "you may not know this, but you can always pass. I mean, you shouldn't pass every time, but it is an option."

Mrs. S. adjusts the zipper on her fanny pack. Elsa takes her turn. Mrs. Staughton says "Thank you" so Faith can go, and then we are done.

DEPLORABLY YOURS

"How'd it go, girls?" Brooke's mom says after we are buckled in.

"Can Kate come over for dinner?" Brooke asks, which is a very diplomatic answer.

"Not on a school night." Then Mrs. Johnson turns on NPR and seems to have forgotten her own question.

When my mom asks, I say it went deplorably. It is kind of a gamble since I haven't had a chance to look up "deplorable" yet.

My mom shakes her head, half smiling. "You have to give Mrs. Staughton a chance. Let her get a few meetings under her belt—"

"Under her fanny pack!" Robin interrupts from the table side of the kitchen.

"You're not helping." My mother hands Robin a stack of napkins. "Mrs. Lawrence is a hard act to follow."

"How'd our friend Nora do?" my dad asks.

"Fine." I decide to save her from any further embarrassment.

I give Rocky his dinner (without being asked) and go up to my room.

de·plor·a·ble
Extremely
unfortunate

The TOWERING VOICE
of my mom

(This is how she
must've looked
when I was a baby.)

My mom says, "Deplorable, huh?"
I look up.

"No more closing circle. No more pod squad leaders. We're having presidents, a different one each month. I got February, which Mrs. Staughton says is important because of the father-daughter dance."

"I was thinking—"

I *know* what she is thinking: "Please do NOT volunteer Dad to take Nora."

"That isn't what I was thinking. How about leaving off the 'father-daughter' and just calling it a dance? Girls can bring their fathers or another special grown-up."

Then Rocky barges in on the conversation. "I'm taking Rocky," I say.

"Uh-oh, something deplorable's happened to deplorable," my mom says, pointing at my dictionary. Rocky's dance has defaced my "department" to "derive" dictionary page.

"There *was* another thing," I say, in case my mom is thinking about leaving the room. "Heather decided that Fall Fun Day is going to be the same Saturday as my sleepover."

"Slumber parties don't usually start until late afternoon, Monkey. We'll work it out." She squats down to mess up my hair. "Hey, if you're not too busy, Fernie could use a little help with her fort downstairs."

"Rocky and I are extremely busy. Did you say something, Mom?" She went straight for my tickle spot.

PRIVATE
and CONFIDENTIAL
The →
LAST Tickle Spot

TWENTy·SIX WAyS

Nora and I say hi to each other on the bus in the morning. It isn't like I sit with her or plan to have her over or anything, but it isn't like it's nothing, either.

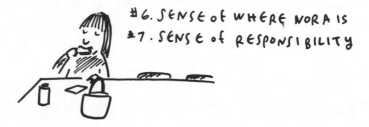

my annoying EXTRA SENSORy PERCEPTION

#6. SENSE of WHERE NORA IS
#7. SENSE of RESPONSIBILITY

Brooke and Eliza agree that having Fall Fun Day on the Saturday of my sleepover is not a big deal. "And if I had to skip one, I'd definitely skip the Fall Fun Day," Brooke says.

"I don't think so. You're president in October," I remind her.

"You two have to promise you won't skip—I wouldn't skip if *you* were president." Eliza and I pinky-swear we won't.

Specials:
A GYM
B HEALTH
C LIBRARY
D COMPUTER
E MUSIC
(FART)

Mrs. Petty's three-word lesson plan is on the TV in her room: self-portrait noses. We are all gathered around for her nose-drawing demonstration. "Are we going to rush right in and scribble a nose?"

Zombie chorus: "NO!"

"We are going to very carefully draw our noses like this."

Before she starts, I raise my hand to make a suggestion: "There is more than one way to draw a nose."

Mrs. Petty smiles and says, "Let's see if we can't all make a nose this way before we start branching out, Katie."

~ START BRANCHING OUT, KATIE ~

She gives us our self-portraits. I can't; I am literally unable to put a nose that does *not* look like my nose *or* my drawing on my so-called self-portrait.

I show Brooke my masterpiece.

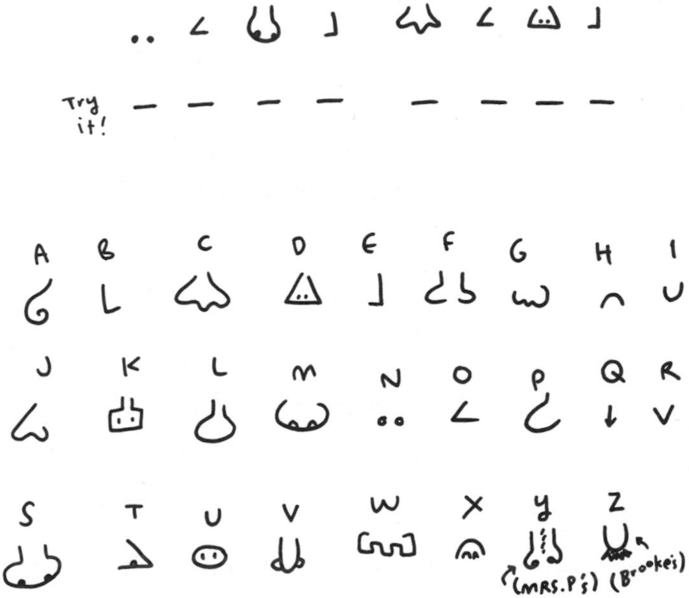

.. ∠ (picture code) ...

Try it!
— — — — — — — —

A B C D E F G H I
J K L M N O P Q R
S T U V W X Y Z
(Mrs. P's) (Brooke's)

Mrs. Petty is very pleased with everyone's nasal progress until she gets to my portrait. "You're Robin Geller's sister, aren't you?" bringing the grand total number of times she's asked me this question to fourteen.

"Robin was a very good art student," Mrs. Petty says sadly, like Robin is dead or has actually gone to live with her biological artist parents. "Why don't you come see me during recess on Monday? . . ."

> Why don't I...
>
> O let me count the reasons why:
>
> 1. Other students are more deserving of your special attention.
> 2. I am medically required to go to recess.
> 3. I would rather drink the paintbrush water.

". . . That way everybody will be on the same page next class."

⌐∨⌐ ⌐.. ⌐⌐⌐ ⌐⌐⌐⊙⌐

— — — ‒ — — — — — —
═══
⌐⌐∪.. ⌐.. ⌐∪⌐

— — — — — — — — — —

⌐⌐⌐⌐ ⌐⌐⌐⌐

— — — — — — — — .

Mrs. Petty collects our papers. She holds up Peter Buttrick's portrait before putting the pile on the shelf.

Hui Zong was supposed to come over on Saturday to work on our Maryland project, but she has a "family obligation." We are mostly caught up, so it was really just an excuse to hang out. I had invited Brooke to hang out with us, but she actually has to stay home to work on her project. It's kind of funny (strange, not ha-ha): I was jealous Brooke was partners with Colin, and now Brooke is jealous I am partners with Hui Zong. I'm not really looking forward to the weekend.

my DREAM PARTNER
COLIN SMITH

Blue eyes
wheaten hair
square chin

my REAL PARTNER
HUI ZONG TIAN

SCREWBALL SATURDAY

"Exciting finish, Champ!" my dad says as we head for my soccer bag on the sidelines.

my FAVORITE PART of the GAME ♫

ICE CREAM

I agree. I mean, it's always exciting to finish soccer.

"One minute to go, Heather scores the tiebreaking goal, and your friend Brooke has the assist! Where did she disappear to? I wanted to congratulate her—"

"Brooke had to leave right away. Her mom said we could have a sleepover if she and Colin are all caught up on their colonial project."

"I'll congratulate her tonight, then," my dad says. "Listen, your mother texted me, seems Mrs.—"

"Adam! Adam!" The red sweat suit is speed-walking toward us.

"Help me out, Champ," my dad says. He is very bad with names.

"Heather's mom, Mrs. Staughton, as in our new Junior Guide leader?"

"Right. First name?"

"Mrs.?"

"Thanks!" He gives my ponytail a yank. "Great game!" he greets Mrs. Staughton.

"Terrific team effort!" says the mother of the star of the game. "Is there any chance I can send Heather home with you two? I've got to run to a coaches' meeting."

"Unfortunately, not this morning—my wife made other arrangements." Dad looks off in the direction of my soccer bag. And then I see the Other Arrangements.

The REVOLUTION of my SATURDAY

BROOKE → HEATHER? → NORA

"No problem," Mrs. Staughton says. "I'll take Heather with me."

"Dad?!"

Take ME with you!

"I started to tell you, your mother texted—Mrs. Klein has a mall event today, and Lexi has an all-day soccer tournament. Mrs. Klein asked if we'd keep Nora until lunchtime."

"Did anybody think about asking me?"

"You mean, 'TIME OUT, COACH DAVE! I HAVE AN IMPORTANT QUESTION FOR KATE!' You were playing soccer. We're talking about a total of an hour of your time, Kate. C'mon, Mom and Nora are waiting."

"Good game, Kate!" My mom gives me a hug. If it weren't for Nora, this would be a special occasion. My mom never comes to games. "I brought your sneakers."

I sit down next to my bag to change my shoes and Nora looks up from her book. "Do you actually like soccer?" she asks.

ILLEGAL
QUESTIONING
on a soccer field
in front of a
soccer-nut dad!

"My dad loves soccer. What are you reading?"

UNNECESSARY
REFERENCE!
(to dad)

"The Witch of Blackbird Pond."

"Me too! Wait, what colony did you get?"

"New Hampshire."

"I have Maryland. Boring," I say.

"Only the boring are bored," my dad says. He hands me money

Nice one, Mr. G!

Bob says...

for the ice cream truck. "Can we get you an Eskimo Pie?" he asks, looking at Nora. It's supposed to be a joke—she's all bundled up like an eskimo.

"Screwball," she says. It's not supposed to be an insult. It's an ice cream.

"Do those still have gum in the bottom? Your mother mentioned something about braces," my mom says.

"Mom, the gumball is all crumbs; it's been frozen for a hundred years. You can't really chew it."

"All right, Gum Police Officer Geller, are we trading cars?" Dad says. "I'll go grab Fern's booster seat."

"Screwball for the screwball?" It's Heather. She and Allie are laughing.

Nora is exchanging her orange screwball for a raspberry one. I can't tell whether she heard what Heather said, so I don't bring it up on the way to the parking lot. Instead I ask her about her braces.

"I have a retainer," she says. She opens her mouth.

Fern's booster is still sitting on top of my dad's car. I look an extra-long time at Nora's rainbow-colored retainer so Nora completely misses the part where my dad is bagging up all the disgusting stuff that piles up under Fern's seat.

"That bag does not go anywhere near my car," my mom says. "Right into the trash! And please, please do not move my files."

"Yes, sir, officer," my dad says. He goes to put a towel down, but Nora has already flopped in on Fern's side of the backseat.

"Are you friends with Heather?" Nora asks while I'm belting in, and then she mutters to her window, "She asks the girl who's friends with everybody. . . ."

"Not exactly," I answer the girl who's friends with nobody.

"Is she invited to your slumber party?"

Another good question. "I'm not sure," I say, and I ask my mom to turn on the radio, which is another synonym for "end of conversation."

"How about a car game instead?" my mom says.

"How about Kiss 108?" Nora says, and my mom actually puts the radio on.

sMALL PROBLEM

"What time are we meeting Nora's mom?" I ask as we pull into the mall's parking garage.

"One-thirty. I have a couple of errands—you girls can grab slices at the food court."

"Pizza gives me acne," Nora says. "We'll go to guest services; I'm sure my mother ordered special lunches—"

"We can't bother your mother today, Nora. It doesn't have to be slices. You girls can get whatever you like at the food court," my mom says.

Nora gets out of the car without answering.

♫ DO YOU SEE WHAT I SEE?

♫ A stain, a stain with a tail as big as a kite!

↳ DETAIL

I pray my mom will say something. It's so embarrassing. Maybe no one will notice. Maybe I should've warned Nora about Fern's side of the seat.

Note to SELF:
BE SPECIFIC
with prayers.
Amen.

"All right, everybody back here, Macy's entrance, at one-thirty," my mom says.

I set my watch alarm for *1:30*. "We have a little extra time. . . ." Here's something you may never hear me say again: "Do you want to go shopping?"

... as in trying on clothes (OFF)

"I hate shopping," Nora says. "Besides, I'm hungry. It's lunchtime—the food court is going to be packed."

I am praying that the Macy's mirrors will say something ABOUT THE STAINS as we cut through on our way to the food court.

MIRROR, MIRROR on the WALL, SHOW NORA the stain for US ALL!

I give it another shot on the escalator. "This place is always so hot," I say, wrapping my sweatshirt around my waist.

I tried, Mrs. Roosevelt.

"I never get hot," Nora says, stuffing her hands in her sweatshirt pockets. It actually pulls the sweatshirt down in front, worsening the situation in back.

All the kiosk people say hi to Nora on our way to the food court—she is a Mall Celebrity. Maybe that's why she doesn't mind being a total loner at school. I have to stop looking to see if anybody is noticing her shorts when she asks me what I am looking at.

NORA the FOOD COURT QUEEN!

Orange Chicken Lady	Trattoria Joe Dude	Cinna BONANZA!
Take 3, Miss Nora.	OLIVES on the PLAIN Slice-it's Nora's pal.	NORA'S USUAL: The Biggest one with extra frosting

Nora is still waiting in the Cinnabon line when my slice is ready, so I pick a table and am considering getting myself another sample of orange chicken when someone puts their hands over my eyes. "Guess who!"

"Brooklet?!" I reach behind my head for her braids. "Are you and Colin all finished?"

"Oh no, no, not even close. He's here somewhere. We're on a project-supply run," she says, and helps herself to the first bite of my pizza. "Hey, there's Nora Klein! A rare mall-sighting . . . what's today? Mark it on your Junior Guide calendar!" Nora is in front of Colin, who is carrying an OfficeMax bag and an Orange Julius.

The First Best Bite

"Actually, Nora comes here all the time. Watch this!" We watch as Nora takes three more samples of orange chicken.

"Miss Nora?!" Brooke imitates the sample lady.

"Her mom works here," I say as Nora puts her Cinnabon on the table, with a ketchup cup full of extra frosting.

"My mom has some work thing today, so the Gellers are babysitting me," Nora says to her tray.

And before anyone can say anything else, Colin says:

"Nora, you have a big brown spot on the bu—back of your shorts."

Nora freezes. Colin tries not to laugh. I can't look at Brooke.

Nora backs out of her seat, leaving her Cinnabon on the table.

"It's chocolate!" I say to Brooke and Colin. "And it's really not that big." And I don't say, "Smell it!"

"How do YOU know?!" Nora says, glaring at me.

SAVED by the

"It's one-thirty! We have to go. Nora's mom—"

I walk backward with Nora until Brooke and Colin and the food court are out of sight.

"Stop for a second. Try this." I yank her sweatshirt way down.

PRESTO

"No, you stop!" she says angrily, pulling away. "You got me back for the not-bringing-the-instrument thing, okay! We're even, or you win, if that makes you feel better!"

NO SHORTS-o!

KATE	NORA
I	I

It takes me a few seconds to get it. "You think I did that? On purpose?" Nora doesn't answer. "You chose to sit on Fern's side of the seat—"

"You chose not to say anything!"

"You were already buckled—"

"You could have said something about THE SPOT!"

"Everything okay?" my mom asks when we walk up, the way she does when she can tell it's not.

"Where's my mother?" Nora asks.

"She's running late. She's going to pick you up at our place."

"I need to see her now," Nora says.

My mom looks at me for an explanation. "Dad didn't put a towel down. . . ." I point to Nora's shorts.

"Oh dear," my mom says. She takes her sweater off and ties it around Nora's waist. "You can change when we get home. Kate will loan you a pair of shorts."

Nora heads toward guest services. My mother hasn't let go of her sweater. "This way, girls," my mom says, and shoos us toward the car.

I sit on top of a plastic bag on Fern's side. Nora inspects every square inch of the other side before she sits down.

AFTERNOON·MARE

Fern is riding her bike in circles around my dad when we pull into the driveway. Nora and my mom go into the house.

"Don't you think you better go in, Champ?" my dad asks.

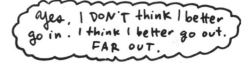

yes. I DON'T think I better go in. I think I better go out. FAR OUT.

My mom comes back out. "Nora's alone in there. . . ."

"She thinks I did it on purpose," I say.

"Did what?" My dad looks at my mom.

"Go in and tell her you didn't." My mom walks me to the garage.

Nora isn't technically alone. Rocky is sitting with her. "I'm sorry," I say, patting Rocky so I don't have to look at Nora. "I'll go get you a pair of shorts."

"I'll go with you," she says, and follows me.

I grab three pairs of shorts from the laundry basket at the top of the stairs. Nora is standing in the doorway of Robin's room gazing up at the horses on the shelf that runs around the top of the room. "This is your room? It used to be such a pigsty."

FOUL!

UNNECESSARY RUDENESS!

I don't say that it is. Or isn't. I hold up the shorts. "Here—you can wear any of these."

"Oh, I don't wear other people's clothes," Nora says, and makes a yuck-face. I am starting to think the silent treatment would be an improvement when she adds, "Skip the shorts, I'll take a horse. That is, if you're really sorry."

"Kate, Nora! Mrs. Klein is here!" my dad yells up from the kitchen.

I stand on Robin's desk and grab the closest horse.

"Seriously?" She puts the horse in her sweatshirt pocket. "Thank you!"

"No big deal," I say, because I don't want her to think it is.

No big deal, no. HUGE DEAL

STOP, come back!

NIGHTMARE

"Seriously?" Brooke says. We are up in my room after dinner. "What were you thinking?! Why didn't you just tell her the horses weren't yours?"

"You must've missed the part where I didn't tell her the room wasn't mine," I say.

"Kate?" my mother calls upstairs. "Come down and say goodbye. Grammalolo is getting ready to leave."

"Oh, Nancy, I don't know why you always make such a big deal of goodbyes. Snickelfritz here hardly had time for hello, she's been so busy with her little friend," Grammalolo says with a fresh lipstick smile, as if I wasn't sitting right next to her all through dinner.

"And please tell your sister Princess Hyacinth I would love it if she'd honor me with an appearance one of these Saturday nights," Grammalolo says.

"Or," my dad says as we watch Grammalolo go down the front walk, "your mother could do the honors and miss her TV show one Sunday night and have dinner with Princess Hyacinth and the rest of us instead."

My mother changes the subject. "Adam, Fern is ready for you to read to her. She can sleep in her own bed, and I'll have these two sleep in Robin's room."

"Ooh, the scene of the crime," Brooke whispers.

"Not funny," I say. (*Translation:* Funny, but stomachache-making.)

I actually forget about the crime while we all watch *America's Funniest Home Videos.*

BROOKE'S and my #1 ALL-TIME DREAM COME TRUE:
GRAND (or ang-) PRIZE WINNERS

AMERICA'S BUNNIEST ♡IDEOS HOME

Then Brooke and I help my mom make Brooke's bed. "Good night," my mom says, and gives Brooke a hug. "I'm glad you and Colin caught up on your project. You two can chat a little longer, but not too late. And I don't need to remind you not to get into anything. This is your sister's room. . . ."

As soon as my mother shuts the door, Brooke says, "You can't leave that hole up there." She stands on the desk and starts rearranging the horses. "Or you might as well put a big sign—"

"Kate?" My mother knocks and opens the door enough to stick her arm in. "Here's your water bottle. Brooke, can I get you one?"

Brooke is shaking her head no, crouching on the desk. "All set, Mom, thanks." My mom shuts the door. Brooke slides off the desk.

"This is a nightmare," I say.

"Night mare," Brooke neighs. And she has to say "Get it?" because I am not laughing. "Look," Brooke says, admiring her work. "I don't think Robin will even notice. It was pretty dusty up there."

We got ready for bed and I had every intention of making it a late night.

KERR-FUFFLE

It turns out Brooke and Colin aren't exactly caught up, so Brooke has to go home right after breakfast. "If you're still planning on marrying Colin," she says, "plan on doing ninety percent of the work."

Brooke calls at four to see if Robin noticed the horse was gone. "She's not home yet," I say. And even though we don't have much to talk about, we end up talking about not much for twenty-seven minutes.

An hour later, Robin gets home from Grace's. "Thanks for setting the table, Katester!" she says. "I'm just going to run upstairs and dump my bag; then I can finish the rest."

RIGHTS   WRONG

"It's all done," I say. "But I'll take your bag up for you, if you want."

She hands me the bag and says, "Is she feeling all right?"

"Kate's been very helpful all day." My mom smiles.

Next morning, two historic firsts: FIRST #1) Nora says hi to me when I get on the bus (before I say hi to her). She may even have smiled. (It's hard to tell; her hoodie covers her mouth.)

I can barely say hi back. Then, FIRST #2) She waits in the bus circle so she can walk with me (and Brooke) into the building.

We are literally just walking, not talking, and Nora walks with us all the way to our lockers. Finally Nora says "See ya," and doubles back to her own locker.

"Is that the—?" Brooke asks.

I nod slowly.

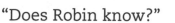

"Does Robin know?"

"Not yet," I say. "I have to get the horse back today."

After morning meeting, Mrs. Block reminds me (and Peter Buttrick) that I will be spending my recess with Mrs. Petty.

Five minutes later, we hear a gag. Mrs. B. says, "Brooke, you better go see the nurse." She hands a hall pass to Brooke. "Do you want to choose someone to walk you down to Mrs. Kerr?"

There aren't a lot of hands. "Kate, why don't you go with Brooke to the nurse's office and come right back?"

Once we are out in the hall, Brooke says, "If you want to get the horse from Nora, you have three options: 1) tell the truth, 2) lie, or 3) steal it, unless you know where we could get a new horse, then there could be a number four."

I shake my head. "I don't even remember exactly what it looks like."

"Then tell Nora the truth and just ask for it back."
Brooke makes it sound easy.

#1. ~~Tell the truth~~ = Admit I already told two lies.
#2. Lie
~~#3.~~ Steal = How I got into this mess.

"Don't think of it as stealing!" Brooke says. "Think of
it as returning the horse to its owner. To the rescue!"
Brooke puts her left hand on her hip with her right
fist outstretched and practically gallops right into
Mrs. Kerr, who is stepping out of the main office.

"I believe one of you is on her way to
see me with a stomachache?" Mrs.
Kerr says.

"Uh, it comes and goes," Brooke says. The whole
horse conversation was actually giving me one, but I
don't say anything.

"I see. Comes and goes." She signs Brooke's pass and returns it. "You can go straight back to class now, girls. I'll tell Mrs. Block you're on your way."

In the hall, I get back to our conversation. "If I took her horse, Nora would say something to somebody*."

"But it's not her horse, Kate!" Brooke says, and we're both quiet until we reach the door. "I guess it's decided, then: option two, lying," she whispers. I feel my face turn red just thinking about it.

*The Somebody Mr. Lovejoy aka "Killjoy"

PRINCIPAL

NOTE: Hands in popular ever. spider-doing-pushups-in-mirror position.

Mrs. Block and Eliza are having another one of their math moments, so Brooke and I slip into our seats. Mrs. Block doesn't say anything to either of us until Brooke hands in her morning math. "Feeling better?" Mrs. Block asks. "Sometimes a little walk with a friend is the best medicine." She winks.

Instead of recess, I go to Mrs. Petty's room. "You caught me!" she says, like it was my idea to drop in. She is eating her lunch. "Now"—she wipes her hands on a paper towel and gives me my portrait paper—"I don't need to keep you all recess, Kate. As soon as you put your nose on there, you may run along."

I may run along, but I can't. Because I may be able to draw a Petty nose in approximately seven seconds, but I can't. I sit there staring at my portrait for eleven minutes.

The ALTERNATIVE:

Watching Mrs.P. eat EGGSALAD

Mrs. Petty walks over and stands behind me. I can see 5B lining up on the playground. I just come out with it. "I can't put your nose on my portrait."

"Kate, art students spend years copying other styles, the Great Masters. That is how you learn."

KATE the GREAT Master

"No offense, but when I make things, I only want to copy what's inside my head."

Mrs. Petty gives up and goes to her desk. She is writing furiously.

I draw my nose. Then I stand, push in my chair, and leave.

What is Mrs. Petty furiously writing?

DETENTION SLIP

NAME: Katie Geller

DATE: Monday

REASON: Insolence.
Insubordination.
Insunasalization.
Petulance. ~~Pestilence.~~ Pettiness.

Mrs. Petty OVER →
SIGNATURE (see attached)

ONLY 168 DAYS until RETIREMENT

Monday

They told me there would be ~~days~~ students like this one and perhaps instead of whining to you, Dear Diary, I should be thanking my lucky stars there is JUST one, whose initials begin with K.G.

HORSE TALES

POSSIBLE LIES

1. Your cousin (who gave you the horse) is coming over and she'll be looking for it.

2. You are going to visit your aunt (who gave you the horse) in the hospital and she asked you to bring it.

3. You have to take it back to the store for a "recall." Apparently, touching the horse can cause warts and other funguses.

I pick option two again, although I am afraid to jinx my aunt, so I plan to leave the hospital part out.

But life does not always go according to plan.

Nora and I say hi and I sit directly behind her on the bus. I don't know which is harder, lying or beginning a conversation with Nora.

Decide fast - we get off at the next stop!

"So last night I was talking with my aunt and . . . ," I begin. "I was wondering if you want to come over."

Silence. I am about to repeat the last part when Nora actually turns around and says, "Are you talking to me?"

I answer yes and she faces forward without saying anything. I am about to ask again, and she says, "I am thinking about it."

That's when Gene looks up in his rearview mirror and says, "Somebody missed her stop."

"Well, there's the answer I was looking for—you can get off at my stop and my dad can take you home."

Emotional
MY WEATHER REPORT

Cloudy with a chance 80%.
of PRECIPITATION

"I have homework," Nora says, which is the same as saying I have ten fingers. In most cases.

Gene waits while I run up the driveway. I drag my dad out so he can give Gene the thumbs-up.

"Nora!" my dad says. He gives her a big one-way hug like he hasn't seen her in months, a little over-the-top even in the extra-fatherly-love department. "Did I know you two—"

"Nora missed her stop," I explain.

"Ahh." He hands Nora the phone when we walk in the house. "Tell your mom I have a conference call in a few minutes, but I can run you home in an hour."

I clear the table so we can do our homework. "Popcorn, anyone?" my dad asks, holding up our popcorn popper.

"You still don't have a microwave?" Nora says.

"Still living in the Stove Age around here," my dad says.

"It tastes better than microwave popcorn," Nora says after my dad sets down her bowl.

"The highest compliment." He bows. "Why don't you two take your popcorn and your homework up to your room, Kate?"

"Never mind," he says, receiving my glare. "Maybe one of these days you'll get that room cleaned up so—"

"Your conference call?" I say.

"Right," he says, and leaves us to our homework.

We work in "silence" until I can't stand it any longer.

131

"So when did you start collecting horses?" I ask.

"Saturday," Nora says.

OPTION #5!

I pause to look down into the horse's eye. "Brownie is used to having his family and a lot of other horses around. I was thinking, you could board him here—that's a horse-word for have him live here. He'd still be yours and everything, but—"

"I think *Victory* is very happy with me. He thinks Brownie is a baby name and he's always wanted to be an only horse, which is something you never understood," Nora says.

She named it Victory?

Nora eats another handful of popcorn and adds, "I think you gave me something and now you're trying to take it back."

We do our homework until my dad comes in. "Shall I leave you two for a bit longer?"

"Well, that was kind of nice," my dad says on the drive home from Nora's. "Maybe we can clear that path through the woods again; this could become more of a regular—"

"This? This was just doing our homework, Dad," I say.

"Well, I'm pretty sure Eleanor Roosevelt is smiling, wherever she is right now." My dad breaks into song: "Kate sera, sera, whatever will be will be, the future is ours to see. . . ." Luckily it's a very short car ride.

ELEANOR
HORSEVELT

Robin lets me hang out in her room until ten while my parents are at their book club.

I am trying to organize Notes to Self, but I am finding it hard to concentrate. It's so obvious the horse is missing.

I'm sure she's noticed, but Robin looks like she's reading A *Separate Peace*. "What's it about?" I ask.

"Are you trying to make conversation, Kate? Because I'm trying to read."

"Sorry. Could I ask you one other thing? I won't interrupt you again." I don't wait for an answer. "If someone has something they're not using, and someone else gives it away to someone who really uses it—would you say that's more like sharing or stealing?"

"What are you talking about, Kate?"

"Taking things people aren't using and giving them to people—"

"Taking other people's things is stealing, Kate," Robin says. "Oh, look, it's ten o'clock!" It's only 9:53. "Bedtime for Kattila!" She hugs me and sends me down the hall.

VICTORy?

On library days, we have exactly twenty minutes to return books and check out new ones, with a grand total of TWO books per person. There are at least fifteen books I would like to take out, so I store them in the biography section. Brooke stores hers by the encyclopedias.

This cuts way down on our book-finding (and checking-out) time so we have way more reading-in-the-beanbag-chair time.

We also have time to play

S TACK·ACK· ATTACK! It's easy! It's fun!

I am stashing two new books while Mrs. Sanelli (a.k.a. Smelly) has her back to me in the Book Nook. "Ack, what's this?"

Brooke sees the whole thing from where she's standing and rushes over. "Smelly has your horse! Nora left it on a beanbag chair. Go claim it!"

"What if Nora comes to look for it?"

"It won't be here. She could've left it somewhere else, or someone could have taken it. . . ."

"Can you, please? Please."

The lost-and-found is outside Mrs. Sanelli's office, behind the checkout desk. Mrs. Sanelli is over by the computers. Brooke cuts to the front of the checkout line. "Excuse me, Mrs. Wright, do you know if anyone's turned in a horse—small, brown, with white feet?"

Mrs. Wright hands Brooke the horse and says, "It was right on top, dear."

"See, you could have done that!" Brooke says as she hands me the horse.

Reasons why Brooke is my Best friend:

12. She'd do anything for me.

We are all working on our colony presentations when we hear knocking (even though the door to 5B is always open). Mrs. Sanelli is standing there like it's shut, so Mrs. B. has to invite her to come in.

"Forgive me for interrupting, Mrs. Block, but may I borrow Brooke Johnson?"

Take ME! Don't take her! She's INNOCENT! Prepare to fall on pencil →

Mrs. Sanelli's lips are smiling, but the rest of her face isn't.

"Brooke?" Everybody watches Brooke cross the room. "You're due back in two weeks!" Mrs. Block says, and smiles.

Twenty minutes go by and there is no sign of Brooke. Mrs. Block arranges the papers on Brooke's desk and says to Colin, "Two weeks—that was supposed to be a library joke."

When the five-minute bell rings, Mrs. B. asks Colin to pack up Brooke's stuff. He has just finished making a neat pile on her desk when Brooke finally walks in.

BROOKE?
LOWS!

✓ 2 braids
✓ 2 eyes
✓ 2 arms
✓ 2 legs
No blood
No tear stains
No stains of any kind
No limp

After the world's longest four minutes, school ends. I am walking backward down the hall, looking into Brooke's face, saying, "I. Am. So. Sorry."

"It's fine," she says.

"Fine? What about Killjoy?"

"He wasn't there. The worst part was right in the beginning when Smelly Sanelli asked me, 'Do you know why I came to get you?'

"Luckily she said, 'Do not answer! You, Nora Klein, and I are going to sit down and get to the bottom of this.' At least I knew it was about the horse.

"Nora was sitting in Smelly's office crying. Mrs. Wright is next to her holding a Kleenex box. And I had to wait outside the office forever until Nora decided she was ready for me to come in.

"So I walked in, and before Smelly could start with her Grand Inquisition, I said, 'Nora, I think I can tell you something that will make you feel a lot better. I found your horse on the beanbag chair in the Book Nook. I gave it to Kate to give to you on the bus.

"Mrs. Wright smiled and winked at me. Nora stopped crying. Smelly was suspicious. She started to say I should've explained all that earlier, but Mrs. Wright said she was busy checking out books."

"Major phew," I say. We're standing in the bus circle, and the buses all start up at once.

"You still have to give the horse back to Nora. Smelly wants a full report from Nora in the morning. Call me!" Brooke says. It takes a few seconds for that to sink in. "You better hurry. Gene is about to shut the doors."

ROUND-UP

"I didn't say anything." I am giving Brooke the full phone report. "I just put it on the seat next to her. She took it and put it in her backpack."

"Did she say thank you?" Brooke asked.

I blow air through my lips like a horse. "No, her exact words were 'Brooke tried to steal my horse. Maybe you should give her one of her own.'"

Robin is standing over me, waiting. "Who are you talking to?"

"Brooke," I mouth.

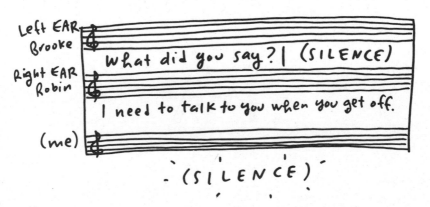

CONVERSATION for TWO EARS

Left EAR Brooke — what did you say? | (SILENCE)

Right EAR Robin — I need to talk to you when you get off.

(me) — (SILENCE)

Robin leaves. Brooke says "Okay" in my phone ear. "She is off the slumber party list. Victory is on!"

"Not funny," I say. (*Translation:* Funny, but discouraging.) The horse project is in a deplorable state. The Nora project is in a ＿＿＿＿＿＿ state.
adj., worse than *deplorable*

After I hang up with Brooke, I go to Robin's room. I am so busy wishing I could talk to her about my deploritude, I forget to wonder why she wants to talk to me in the first place. She shuts the door. Neither of us sits down.

"So, one of my horses is missing."

I look up at the shelf, like someone who doesn't already know.

"I don't know exactly how long it's been gone. I just noticed tonight," she says. "I want to make sure you know I don't think you took it, but Mom mentioned you and Brooke slept in my room—"

"You told Mom?"

"No, this is between you and me—"

"And Brooke. Brooke didn't steal your horse!"

O MR. HORSE. Why the LONG FACE?

Is someone's nose GROWING?

I start to leave, but Robin has her hand on the door. "I've never had to say this to you before. My room is off-limits to you and your friends when I'm not in it."

Ow! "Oh. So it's on-limits now?" I mumble, and then I leave.

Robin shuts the door hard after me.

ROCKY'S ROOM
(♥ unlimited)

IF WISHES WERE HORSES

Brooke goes right up to Nora when she gets off the bus. "You have your horse?" she asks.

Nora turns around so Brooke can see it peeking out of her backpack. Brooke pretends to make a grab for it behind Nora's back, and I feel like I could smile for the first time in a day. I am dying to tell Brooke that Robin knows, but Nora won't leave us alone.

"Don't you have to give Smelly, I mean Mrs. Sanelli, the full report?" Brooke asks Nora after we pass the stairs to the library. Nora doesn't say anything; she just turns around. "Wait, I'll go with you!"

According to Brooke, the full report is not even worth reporting. Mrs. Sanelli made her promise never to claim things that were not hers from the lost-and-found.

We're standing in the foursquare line at recess. "Robin knows the horse is gone."

"Does she think you did it?"

"She thinks *you* did it." It's
my turn to play and I lose on
purpose. Brooke wins and
she ends up staying in for
the rest of recess.

"I wish I did do it," Brooke says once we're lined up
to go in from recess. "Then I'd just give it back. The
whole thing would be over already." She puts her
hand on my shoulder. "You have to tell the truth—"

much much
I'd rather be the person
they think I am:

I don't think
you took it.

ROBIN

Your room
USED to be such
a pigsty.

NORA

"I can't. Can we please talk about something else
instead?"

"Your slumber party?" Brooke says.

"Yes, please!"

"I know, I know—you invite Nora AND Victory. She brings Victory and Robin catches her red-handed and—"

"That's not talking about something else! Besides, Nora won't come."

"We still have four weeks. Four weeks to help her change her mind."

At band practice, Brooke doesn't waste any time getting started. "Rests are for resting QUIETLY, flutes," Mr. Bryant says, holding his finger to his lips. "My section leader, LEADER Co-LEADER no less!"

I whip my head up—not guilty!—and I see he's looking at Nora and Brooke, who may be trying not to laugh but it is not working.

"Hold your horses! Trumpets, you're running away with it." Mr. Bryant stops again. I glance over at Brooke. She didn't even hear the "horses"; she's busy reading something Nora wrote on her notepad.

Brooke waits while I put away the music stand. "Seems like you and Nora had a really good time," I say.

"Oh yeah, well, compared with yesterday . . . ," Brooke says. Then she looks at me. "You're not jealous—!"

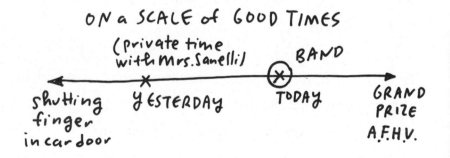

"Jealous of Nora Klein?! Thanks a lot!"

"Because I was only working on your project."

FUN PLANNING

Brooke and I are the first ones at Junior Guides. "Girls, come help me decorate these fruit pizzas!" Mrs. Hallberg says as she sprinkles the grape "olives" on top of the crushed pineapple "cheese."

HOW to MAKE A FRUIT PIZZA

(if you have an hour)

AKA → Grown-up Trick #57 to get kids to eat fruit

blueberry OR grape (olives)

strawberry (pepperoni) slices

cream cheese frosting

crushed pineapple (hide more fruit here.)

baked sugar cookie dough crust

Mrs. Staughton pats my shoulder and says, "You were awfully kind to give Nora that horse. It's nice to see her with her nose out of a book for once! Not that I have anything against reading, of course." She disappears into her fanny pack and pulls out a pizza cutter. "Let's see if we can get twelve slices—nine for you girls, and don't forget your leaders!"

Before Mrs. Staughton turns the meeting over to President Heather, she has a "few words" to say about this year's Fall Fun Day. "I know in the past we've hosted this day for the preschoolers, but this year, I have spoken with the nursing home and everybody loves the idea of holding it there."

(IN CASE you're also wondering where she comes up with them.)

"Mrs. Staughton." I might have forgotten to raise my hand. "Remember when you said you would need our help to make this the best year possible? I would like to offer my help, which is that we should stick with the old Fall Fun Day. My sister Fern is really looking forward to it."

Everyone else with little brothers and sisters agrees.

Mrs. Hallberg is looking at Mrs. Staughton, who is straightening some paper that doesn't need straightening. Then Mrs. S. straightens herself up and says, "Thank you, Kate. Course correction, or we'll stay the course—carry on with the tiny tots. Heather, do you want to take it from here?"

Heather wants us to pair up with someone new for Fall Fun Day planning. (By that she means different, since everyone except Nora has been a Junior Guide since first grade.) Heather pairs herself up with her best friend, Allie. Eliza takes Nora, so I pair myself up with Brooke.

We make a list of Fall Fun Day activities.

(It has been the same list for thirty-three years.)

JUMPY HOUSE
FACE PAINTING
BAKE SALE
DUCK POND
BEAN BAG TOSS
RAFFLE

"What about something really fun, like a corn maze? Or one of those dunking machines? Or a palm reader. Or I know! I know! A haunted house!!!"

Heather listens to Nora's ideas and then writes "costume parade" on the list. Mrs. Hallberg steps in. "All wonderful ideas, Nora. Unfortunately, well . . . you'll understand much better after your first one."

"My last one," Nora mutters.

WHO KNEW?! NORA is a FOUNTAIN of FUN!

BEFORE   AFTER

Heather uncaps the red marker and writes

POD 429 PIZZA PARTY ☺

Allie, Lily, Elsa, and Faith are clapping. "Commemorate and celebrate!" Mrs. Staughton says, adding her claps.

Eliza is looking at me. Nora is looking at the table. And Brooke has the death grip on my leg.

Brooke says, "Invite everybody to your party. You have no choice."

"Now?" I gulped. So I say, "My birthday party is the same day, well, same night as Fall Fun Day. It's a slumber party, and I wasn't planning to send the invitations out for a couple weeks, but the whole pod is invited."

Heather says, "This IS going to be the best Fall Fun Day ever. A Pizza Slumber Party at Kate's house!"

"Kate." Mrs. Staughton is pulling her sweat jacket down over her fanny (not the pack). "Do you want to check with your parents first?"

"Oh, they already know," I say, and smile weakly.

I haven't checked about the pizza, but I've had pizza at every birthday party, except when I turned one.

The closing circle ends super-fast because Fern runs up and hugs me from behind.

FERN'S "TREE" HUG as in "TIM-BER!"

"Your sister saved Fall Fun Day from going to the nursing home," Mrs. Hallberg says to Fern so my mom can hear.

"I invited the whole pod," I tell my mom as we walk to the car.

"Does this have something to do with the nursing home?"

"It has to do with my slumber party. Pod 429 plus Hui Zong. That's ten."

"Are you counting Nora?"

"Yeah, but I'm not counting on her coming. Remember, she doesn't do . . ."

"I'm coming," Fern says.

"You'll be there, Peanut, but it's a party for older girls," my mom says. "Have you thought about what you want to do at your party, Kate?"

"Things you do at slumber parties." I've only been to one, after a pool party, and we were all so tired we actually went to sleep. I don't want mine to be like that.

"It's been a very long time since I went to my last slumber party. You'll have to consult with your sister Robin."

Consulting is OFF- LIMITS.

"What's a slumber?" Fern asks.

"Slumber is sleep," I tell her.

"A sleep party?" she says. "That sounds boring."

UP-n-DOWN

Hui Zong is coming over so we can finish our Maryland project for Monday. We've decided to make a model of the port of Baltimore.

This is Hui Zong's first time making salt dough and I can't talk her out of tasting it.

SALT DOUGH
2 cups flour
1 cup salt
3/4 cup water
2 tsp. vegetable oil

BLECH!

PLUS one Hock
HUI-SPIT (optional)

While the port is baking, we make the ships, ducks, and buildings. Hui Zong cuts a lot of grass, and I suggest broccoli for the trees.

"Won't they smell?" she asks.

"Not if we don't cook them."

Dad is in and out of the kitchen a hundred times. (*Translation:* His writing is not going well.)

It takes way longer than we thought to make the port.

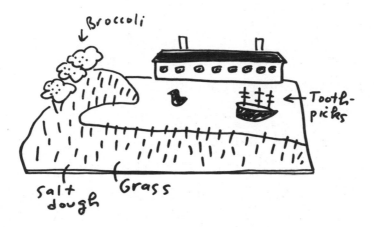

↓ Broccoli

← Tooth-picks

salt dough

Grass

We leave it in the laundry room to dry and go up to my room to work on our report.

Lord Baltimore Sr., Jr., III, and IV (played by Hui Zong) are going to tell the history, including how we Marylanders generously gave our land to make the nation's capitol, Washington, D.C., in 1791. Then I, Kit, am going to talk about a typical day in the life of colonial Marylanders, including the Indians.

colonial
KIT ≛ KATE
(nickname for
Katherine
in colonial times)

"I was thinking Kit and Lord Baltimore should have a scene together at the end," Hui Zong says.

"Nothing romantic," I say, just making sure. "Maybe a scene at the port."

Hui Zong writes the first line of this last scene: "Ahh, this port we call Baltimore."

We go on like that for two sides of a page. I write "The End." Then Hui Zong and I do our Maryland handshake.

After dinner, Dad grabs Bob and picks. "'I always tell the truth,' Stella replies. 'Although I sometimes confuse the facts.'" It's by another Katherine, Katherine Applegate. "It's one of yours, Kate."

My face is red. I put that in, back when I used to tell the truth.

Robin comes in and sits on the edge of the tub while I finish going to the bathroom. "Nora was at the field hockey tournament today." Robin is looking at me; I'm not sure why. Nora is always at the field hockey tournaments. "Nora took my horse. She had it with her."

"Maybe she has one just like it," I say. "I mean, she wouldn't steal your horse and then play with it in front of you."

"I can get Mom to talk to Mrs. Klein—"

"Please don't. I'll talk to Nora," I say. "Can I please have some privacy?"

"If you're so concerned with privacy, you and your friends should keep out of my room!"

L-O-N-G DAY

TO DO:
1. Tell Nora
2. Maryland report
3. Bob
4. Tell Robin
5. Party invitations?
6. HW
7. Practice flute
8. ~~Feed Rocky breakfast~~
9. "   "   dinner

It's the first week of October. We have only been in school for one month. Babies are brand-new when they are one month old, but there is nothing new about school. Maybe school months are like dog years—all I know is this is going to be an extra-long day.

HYGIENE!! *Some things NEVER get old.*

"Hi, Gene!" I say. I sit behind Nora and tap her sweatshirt shoulder. "I was thinking, do you want to come over today, on purpose? We can do homework, if you want."

"Popcorn?"

"Definitely."

Nora walks Brooke and me to our lockers.

"Robin saw her with the horse at field hockey," I tell

Brooke. "Now she thinks Nora stole it."

"Ta-da! I'm innocent!" Brooke slams her locker shut. "Sorry. What're you going to do?"

"Tell Nora the truth. She's coming over after school."

"Ooh, bet you can't wait!" Brooke says.

"Morning, girls! New seating chart today! Upside-down horseshoe—it's a symbol of good luck!" Mrs. Block greets us at the door. It takes a minute to find my desk. "You're with your colonial buddy—perfect for today's presentations!"

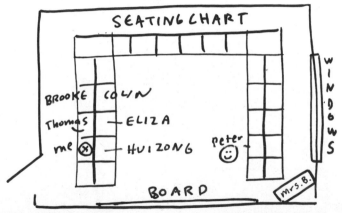

Colin and his mother walk in next, lugging his colonial project. "OH NO!" I say.

I go to Mrs. Block's desk. "I left my project at home. Can I please call my dad?" Our school has a strict policy about kids forgetting assignments. "I know, it is my responsibility and I have to accept the consequences, but Hui Zong should not. It's her project, too. Please?" Mrs. B. hands me the phone.

ASAP! And please wear shoes NOT slippers real pants NOT sweats and a woul your hair hurt. Thanks. Dad. HURRY!

I have a hard time concentrating on everyone else's report until Mrs. B. gets the call from the office.

Mrs. B. skipped Maryland while I was gone, and Brooke and Colin are literally in the middle of Boston's Freedom Trail when I return.

I kind of want to laugh. Everyone else is, but I can't see Brooke's face. Then I hear her snort, and I can't help myself. Mrs. Block helps the two of them up. "Hui Zong and Kate, you're next. Why don't you get ready while I make some repairs to the Freedom Trail," she suggests.

Our report begins well. The Lord Baltimore and Kit parts go exactly like we practiced them.

Then on Lord Baltimore's cue: "Ahh, this port we call Baltimore . . ."

I take off the lid and hold up the port.

"How does it feel looking out on all of this, all . . . all ruined by my dog?!" I am considering crying when I hear Brooke snort again.

Hui Zong is very professional. She doesn't miss a line. And Mrs. B. is very professional. She says, "I am impressed with how my fifth graders are rolling with the unexpected this morning."

We change into our regular clothes. "I am so, so, so, so-to-the-thirty-ninth sorry, Hui Zong," I say.

"That's okay, Kate. It doesn't change my opinion of your dog." She makes a bad face. "And it doesn't change my opinion of you." She puts out her right hand and we do the Maryland handshake.

After Thomas and Eliza wrap up their Virginia report, we go to lunch.

Brooke is removing the soggy "lettuce" from her sandwich. Eliza is buying chocolate milk. My to-do list is running through my head.

"If I invited the whole pod to my birthday party, do I still need to send invitations?"

TO DO:
1. Tell Nora
2. ~~Maryland report~~
3. Bob
4. Tell Robin
5. Party invitations?
6. HW
7. Practice flute
8. ~~Feed Rocky breakfast~~
9. " " dinner

"Totally," Brooke says. "If you want presents. Or else the parents might think it's a Junior Guide thing, like a Fall Camp-In or something."

"Maybe *that's* what we should do, camp for my slumber party—"

"Nora?" Brooke says.

"I thought she was off the list," Eliza says. We spot Nora eating her lunch at her usual table.

"We're trying to get her back on. . . ." Brooke stops and looks at me. "Aren't we?"

I nod. It kind of depends on what happens this afternoon, but Eliza doesn't know anything about the horse project.

"Then we should ask her to sit with us," Eliza says. "She is actually funny. I like being her partner in Junior Guides."

The Nora I know would sit with us if she felt like it, but I suppose it wouldn't hurt to ask.

Brooke returns to party planning. "I think you've got to go with a Halloween theme, Kate." And that's as far as we get because our table is dismissed for recess.

LATER (SAME LONG DAY)

I am sitting behind Nora again.

"You told your mom about coming over?" I ask, and the hood nods.

The truth is about to come out. But not on the bus. "I don't suppose I could interest you in helping to plan a party you're not planning to come to," I say after a while.

"Who said I wasn't coming?"

Excuse me? "I don't do birthday parties?!" I say, and stop myself from imitating her snoring.

"Oh, that was before," she says.

At our house, my dad gives Nora another big greeting. And this time Rocky comes up with one, too. I stand back.

"Dad, did you notice anything unusual about Baltimore before you put it in the box?"

Rocky is sitting beside Dad and the two of them are looking at me innocently.

"He," I say, pointing at Rocky, "ruined it."

"I think he— Well, *we* paid for it. He must've had six bowls of water and gone out five times last night. Salt dough—nasty stuff!" My dad rubbed Rocky's belly. "Bring the port home, we'll restore it."

"It's in the dumpster."

"Then I suggest you two make up and move on," my dad says.

I take Rocky into the laundry room. We look each other in the eyes and I say "Never again" as we shake. Trouble with Rocky is, it's always something, and it's never the same thing twice.

Formerly
Known as

Dad's Best
Running Shoe

The Ol'
Lidless

Kitchen Trash

Back in
the days of

Indoor plants

When I go back into the kitchen, Nora and my dad are talking quietly.

"Listen, Champ, what do you think about having a haunted house for your slumber party? You're turning ten, double digits, this could be the year...." Nora gives it two thumbs-up.

It has a Halloween theme and extremely good potential to keep everyone up all night. "Just not too scary," I say.

"What's TOO scary?" he says.

"Your dad is so different from mine," Nora says.

"My dad is different. Period." I hesitate. "Do you miss yours?"

"It's easier not to," she says, which I take to mean that she does.

"Um, speaking of easier not to . . . I have to tell you something."

Nora puts Victory-Brownie on the table.

"He belongs to my sister," I say.

"Yes! I knew it!" she says like it's some big victory (with a small *v*). "I knew that wasn't your room! Your dad said that thing about cleaning your room last week; then Robin wanted to see my horse on

Saturday. But taking your sister's horse seemed like something I would do . . . not you. Not perfect Kate Geller. I knew you weren't telling the truth."

WHAT A TANGLED WEB WE WEAVE

You you & didn't want I WAS really you thought
said if, your mom I lied. SORRY the horses
my was really I don't were
room was really was know mine.
Pigsty there. why.

WHEN FIRST WE PRACTICE TO DECEIVE.
—Sir Walter Scott, ~~Arachnophobe~~ Novelist

I don't say anything at first.

"Sorry. Mostly," I eventually say. "The truth is, I gave you the horse because I wanted to make you feel better. I never said Robin's room was mine. You thought it was. So you thought the horses were mine. And I never corrected you. It was easier not to. That's the other truth."

"It figures," Nora says. "You're even a nice liar."

"Thanks?" While we're making popcorn, I ask Nora how her New Hampshire report went.

"I hate giving reports in front of the whole class."

"Brooke fell down during hers—"

Nora starts laughing. "How?"

"She and Colin were standing inside these big scroll-tubes unrolling the history of Boston and they both went down."

Nora says, "I always laugh when people fall. Can't help myself. And sometimes it's not funny."

We do our homework in comfortable, truthful silence until a little after five. "Girls, girls, I'm going to have to ask you to keep it down in here—

a man can't work with all the racket and goings-on!" My dad's idea of a joke about silence.

"It's time for me to take Ninotchka home."

"Nora, please," Nora says. "I haven't been Ninotchka since I was four." She puts her homework away and zips her backpack.

"I'll be out in the garage coming up with a new nickname," my dad says.

The horse is still sitting on the table.

"Victory?" I ask Nora. She moves it toward me.

"Thanks," I say.

"No big deal," Nora says. I put the horse in my backpack in case Robin gets home while we're gone.

STELLA by CANDLELIGHT

It's not easy talking about the truth when you haven't told the whole truth. I go first to get it over with.

> "I always tell the truth," Stella replies. "Although I sometimes confuse the facts." Katherine Applegate

"This was my favorite sentence from *The One and Only Ivan*. I can't remember exactly what it used to mean, but I've thought a lot about the truth since yesterday." I cannot look at Robin.

"I think Stella is saying it's not a lie when you believe you are telling the truth. That made me realize it *is* a lie when you know you are *not* telling the truth, even if you aren't saying anything at all."

"I think you're talking about a lie of omission," my mom says. "It's basically a failure to tell the truth."

me

fail·ure
1. Not performing as expected or asked
2. One who fails

"Who is Stella?" Fern asks.

"An elephant," I answer.

"A talking elephant?"

"Sort of," I say. "She can only talk to other animals, not people."

"I thought the quotes had to be by people," Robin says. "Someone who confuses facts might be a nice person, but I wouldn't trust them with the truth. The truth is all about the facts." She stares at me.

"The fact is it's a school night," my mom says. "This is a topic we can revisit on another night."

"Wait, one question!" Fern says. And we all wait for her to say, "Never mind, I forget."

My dad passes Bob to me. "I remember," Fern says. "Do animals lie?"

"Great question!" My dad's already written it down and popped it into Bob. I make sure not to pick it.

"What if?"

"That's the very first one I ever put in there," my dad says, looking at it like it's somebody's baby picture or something.

I put on my pajamas, then go downstairs and pretend to do my homework until Robin goes up to her room. I wait ten minutes, then follow her. The door is closed. It feels weird, but I knock.

She opens the door and I hand her the horse.

"What did she say?" Robin asks.

"Can I come in?" She lets me in and we just stand there. "She didn't say anything." The truth is caught in my throat, so I have to clear it. A couple times.

"I gave Nora your horse. It doesn't matter why.

"And I should have told you before. I'm sorry."

Robin doesn't say anything. She goes to her desk and moves her homework so she can put her horse back. I ♡̸ HORSES.

"Are you going to tell?" No answer. "Are you going to say anything?" No answer. I leave and the door shuts behind me.

PARTY PLANNING

The next morning on the bus, Nora puts her backpack on her lap and says "How did it go with Robin?" before either one of us says hi.

HISTORIC FIRST I sit down next to her.

"She's not talking to me at the moment," I say. "But we're sisters . . . we'll get through it."

"You're lucky your sister's like that," she says.

When we come in from lunch-recess, everybody's desk has the same newspaper article on it.

4 ARRESTED IN COLUMBUS DAY PROTESTS

The local Columbus Day parade was interrupted this Monday morning as bands of protestors hosted sit-ins at key places along the route, including in front of City Hall. Hundreds of protestors camped out all night to make their voices heard. Together, they rejected the celebration of Columbus Day. They denied that Columbus discovered the Americas, instead emphasizing the importance of Native Americans who inhabited the land before 1492.

When the police approached the group, they began waving homemade banners and chanting in unison. The four leaders were promptly arrested for disturbing the peace, and the crowd of protestors quickly dispersed. As a result of this incident, the parade was delayed for multiple hours but rolled successfully in the early afternoon.

"Before anybody reads the article, let's talk about the headline," Mrs. Block says. "Why would someone protest a Columbus Day parade?"

Peter raises his hand. "It started at five a.m. It was really, really long and everyone had to watch standing up. No chairs were allowed. No candy throwing. And there were fifty speeches plus it was hot, at least eighty-five degrees."

Why I wouldn't last long as a TEACHER

(A head can only hold
so much laughter in.)

Mrs. Block smiles and acts like those are answers. Then she calls on Thomas. "The people who were arrested believe we shouldn't celebrate Columbus Day because Columbus didn't really discover America. The Native Americans were already here."

Don't Use these words Dictionary "Essential for teachers"

"Exactly," Mrs. Block says. "Now, on the ⟨backside⟩ of your article, you will see that I have given each of you a new identity.

"We don't have school on Columbus Day, but 5B will be holding a very special class celebration next Friday afternoon. A celebration you will be planning and preparing together . . . using your new identities."

She rolled a wagon full of library books into the middle of the room. "Please use at least one primary source and two secondary sources when you are researching your new identities. You may begin."

I'm the Real Thang.
PRIMARY SOURCE

I used . . .
SECONDARY SOURCE

"Who'd you get?" I ask Brooke while we're waiting at the book wagon.

"Rigaberto Menchu."

Rigoberta Menchu

← Nobel Peace Prize

Peace activist, politician, indigenous Guatemalan
* Only 15 women have won the Nobel Peace Prize.

"Never heard of him. I'm Columbus!" I whisper.

Starring
KATE Geller
as
Christopher Columbus

Thomas Bergen is Franklin Roosevelt. I can already see this is going to be way more interesting than the egg carton ships we made for last year's Columbus Day project.

I did not say it was going to be the best Columbus Day project ever, which I now know is a jinx. But apparently "way more interesting" is also a jinx.

Born in Italy·Cristoforo Colombo
Spanish · Cristóbal Colón
English · Christopher Columbus
Lived 1451-1506.(My secondary source says people didn't care which country they were from until the late 1700s.)

REALITY COULD USE A LOT MORE IMAGINATION...

IMAGINATION	REALITY
What color balloons do you want to have at our party, Christopher?	Are we going to spend another 20 minutes insulting Columbus OR are we going to come up with our own day?!

I have to drag Brookoberta Menchu out of social studies to go to band. And then I have to beg her to be Brooke, her real identity. We get to band a few minutes late and guess what? We do not need our instruments. Everyone except Nora has theirs. "I swear I didn't know until this morning," she says.

We are going to be counting and clapping for the next half hour, if we do not die of boredom first.

COUNT - CLAP . . .

CORRECT: 3 and 4 E . and . A

NORA: One *crap I mean* SNAP!

BROOKE: 3 and 4 E and A | SNORT.

Then Brooke adds the snort, and pretty soon the three of us are laughing so hard I can't count anymore, either.

PRESIDENT JOHNSON

Nora beat us to the cafetorium. I don't know what I expected.

I **do** know what I expected...

FALSE!!

"HI, KATE!"

Broken-the-Big-Laugh-Barrier
NORA

N͟OT

Same ol'
NORA

She is reading her book across from Mrs. Hallberg (which is better than reading in the back corner), who is arranging vegetables and dip. "Runaways!" Mrs. Hallberg exclaims as she dumps the mini-carrots and two roll off the platter. Nora puts them on the platter, never taking her eyes off her book.

The BIG Mini-carrot QUESTION:
??? ARE THEY...???

OR

really BABIES

pieces of OLD CARROTS
not fit for a PIG

183

Today is Brooke's first meeting as pod president. Mrs. Staughton makes a formal ceremony out of the Passage of the President's Notebook. We all clap for Heather's service in September, although this guinea pig is not sorry to see her go.

Heather ends up sitting next to me, where Brooke usually sits, since Brooke has to sit by Mrs. Staughton. Then Heather ends up being my poster partner and Brooke gets to work with Nora.

"The president shouldn't have to work with Nora," Heather says. "There should be a law about that in the binder."

"Nora's okay," I say.

Mrs. S. announces, "Mrs. Hallberg and I are passing out poster board and markers."

MRS. H. and MRS. S. ARE PASSING OUT...

THe MOMENT LOST ON HEATHER, NOT LOST hereby FOREVER.

"Okay," Heather says. "Fall Fun Day. Maybe we have some fall leaves having some fun!"

"Maybe," I say. Kind of obvious, but I guess it doesn't have to be the World's Best Idea. This isn't a contest or anything; we just need to come up with a poster.

"Great! You're such a good artist, you can draw it . . . since I thought of the idea and everything," Heather says. *Translation:* You do the work. I'll go hang out with my friends.

After we finish our posters, Mrs. Staughton has yet another new idea for closing circle. "How about we face the Guide to our left and say, 'Guide's name, I'm so glad you came to Guides today because blank." She looks at us.

"I'll start," I say.

what I want to say:

> Guide's name, I'm so glad you came to Guides today because blank.

what I really say:

> Heather, I'm so glad you came to Guides today because you gave me a compliment on my art.

Mrs. Staughton adds, "Compliments fill our wells."

Heather turns and says, "Allie, I'm so glad you came to Guides today because you had an orthodontist appointment and I didn't get to eat lunch with you."

Allie says to Brooke, ". . . because Heather doesn't have to be president anymore." She didn't mean it like I would have.

Brooke says to Nora, ". . . because you made me laugh really hard. Again!"

Nora has Mrs. Hallberg and everyone is wondering whether she will pass. "I'm so glad—"

Mrs. Staughton interrupts to correct her: "Mrs. Hallberg, I'm so glad . . ."

Nora keeps going: "You came today because I love vegetables."

Brooke does a cover-up cough-laugh. Mrs. Hallberg smiles and takes her turn.

On our way out of the cafetorium, I ask Brooke, "How is it being president?"

"More like secretary or something. Doing attendance, copying stuff, taking notes."

"You were in charge of cleanup. Mrs. S. didn't even set her alarm."

Brooke shrugged. "You know, though," she says, "I think the Nora Project is totally working out." It's true. We high-five. When I think about it, Nora didn't even seem like a project today.

My mom and Fern are waiting in front of the school. We honk as we drive by the Kleins' car and my mom says, "I keep meaning to tell Mrs. Klein I can bring Nora home. No sense in both of us driving."

"Mom, I think Nora's going to come to my party," I say. "I don't know if we're what you would call friends exactly, but we had an excellent time in band today— I mean, band was boring, but Nora, Brooke, and I had fun. And I sat with her on the bus this morning."

"Kate, that's terrific," my mom says.

"Congratchlations!" Fern says. And I tickle her.

"Anything going on with you and your sister?" my mom asks, and she doesn't mean Fern, who's now trying to tickle me. "As Dad said, the tension's so thick you could cut it with a baby fork."

"She didn't tell you?" I say.

"I know nothing, I see nothing, I hear nothing," my mom says.

As we walk into the kitchen, my dad is waving the oven mitt over a sheet full of smoky taco shells. "Forgot to take the paper out. . . . How was everyone else's day?"

Robin is setting the table. "Thanks for not telling, Rob," I say.

"Special leniency for first-time offenders," she says. Whatever that means. "Just don't do it again."

BEHOLD the 16 FORK!

(I don't care if it's a no-fork night!)

ALL IS FORKIVEN!
(Please forkive the pun.)

O-N-O-NOT THIS AGAIN-O-R-A

There is no "Hi, Kate!" from Nora this morning. She is reading on the bus, the one place I have never seen her read before.

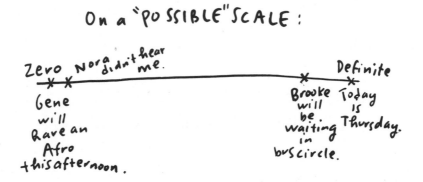

On a "POSSIBLE" SCALE:

Zero — Nora didn't hear me.

Gene will have an Afro this afternoon.

Brooke will be waiting in bus circle.

Definite

Today is Thursday.

It is possible she did not hear my "Hi, Nora!" So I try again from my seat. "What are you reading?"

Nothing.

At lunch, Brooke says, "Well, we knew she was weird already. Not that it changes anything."

She didn't even say "hi."

weird.

I don't feel like saying jinx.

Nora says nothing on the way home, either. And another grand total of nothing on Friday.

NOTHING aka The Emptiness · Nada · Zero Zip · Zippo · Zilch · Big Goose Egg naught · Bupkis · Nil · Null · Nix Diddly squat or just plain squat

My dad is waiting for me in the driveway. "Can I interest you in a trip to the hardware store?"

I spin around. "Are you talking to me?"

"I had an excellent idea for your haunted house. If I put it together over the weekend, I can show Nora on Monday."

"Oh, that won't be happening," I say.

"She has other plans?"

"I doubt it, but it's hard to know. She stopped speaking to me again."

"What did you do this time? Sneeze?"

"I have no clue."

"Sorry to hear that, Champ. Did you ask her why she stopped talking?"

"I don't think answering questions is part of her not-talking plan."

"Right. Silly question. It's just that sometimes people do things to get you to pay extra attention. So nothing happened between you two. . . ."

"Dad, this really was not my day."

"Oh. Well, that happens sometimes—there's been a mix-up. Probably some kid in Topeka, Kansas, who got your day by mistake is saying the same thing to her dad at this very minute."

also AT THIS VERY MINUTE TOPEKA, KANSAS, KID IS *also* WISHING for a MOUTH-SIZE PIECE of DUCT TAPE.

"Dad!"

He pulls my head to his chest.

"What else?" he asks.

"I don't know why Mrs. Block made me Columbus. I thought she liked me. Brooke and everybody else get to be indigenous people who celebrate their own cultures, the ones they think I wiped out. And they all like their new identities. I am the only one who can't wait to be my regular self when class is over."

"I'm sure Mrs. Block thought you could handle it," my dad says. "There must be other people who are on your—I mean, Columbus's side."

"Peter Buttrick doesn't count. He's the president of an Italian American foundation and wants to make Columbus Day some kind of Italian American celebration. Thomas Bergen is Franklin Roosevelt, who made the stupid holiday official. The king and queen of Spain are completely out of it. Eliza is this Ann Rand person who — I really like Eliza, but I do not want Ann Rand on my side."

Ayn Rand

Russian-born Novelist · philosopher

193

"Mrs. Block has you studying Ayn Rand?"

"Ann Rand says Europeans are better than Indians, as if it's a proven fact, and they don't deserve a parade."

"Oooh. Sounds worse than being Columbus," my dad says. "C'mon, how 'bout the hardware store and some frozen yogurt?"

A FEW of MY FAVE
Hardware Store Things

SKITTLES
machine

The
SMELL

PAINT
CHIPS

"Deal."

My dad is driving home with his elbow out the window. We have managed not to talk about Nora or my day for the entire time.

GOIN' DOWN the open-window ROAD...

SOME PEOPLE'S HAIR IS MEANT for IT.

And SOME PEOPLE'S EARS are MEANT for IT.

Dad, can you put the window up?

Huh? Hold on, Kate—lemme put my window up.

The car seems extra quiet. "I've been thinking about Nora," my dad says, smoothing his hair. "You're going to have to find another way to communicate. Of course, I'm a big fan of writing, but I'm sure there are other ways."

Call me uncreative, but I couldn't think of another way.

I spend too much of Sunday lying on my bottom bunk bed trying to write the perfect note to Nora. The one that would make us be friends, or whatever we were, again.

SINGING GORILLA

" ♫
"

MORSE CODE
.... ..

FRIENDSHIP HERBS

NOSE CODE
∩ ∪

Bunkered down...

I tiptoe to Robin's room for the first time since I gave the horse back, which isn't even a week but it feels like a year. I am standing there forever, so eventually I tap her door extremely lightly and she jumps. "Kate, don't do that!"

I say "Sorry," even though it's not really my fault. "Would you please read this?"

> Dear Nora,
>   Since you are not talking to me, I am not asking you out loud, but I would really like to know why not. I am hoping you will write the reason here: _____
> _____
> _____
>   I was beginning to think we were friends. I miss you.
>   Kate

"Do you want my honest opinion? It's good, but I think you should copy it over so she can't see all the stuff you erased. Are you going to mail it to her?"

my INVENTION IDEA:
The DO you WANT to KNOWer

Tells you if you want to know something BEFORE someone tells you.

"I was planning to drop it on her lap on the bus."

"What if she doesn't answer? I could talk to Lexi, see if she knows anything," Robin offers.

"Thanks, but I doubt it." I start to leave.

"Hey, have you seen my eraser collection?"

"I didn't take it!"

She holds a box out. "I meant have you ever seen it? I found it in my desk the other day; I don't think it's been opened since I was in sixth grade. Want it?"

"Thanks," I say, and open the box.

"Sorry about Nora," she says.

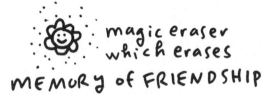

magic eraser
which erases
MEMORY of FRIENDSHIP

NEGATIVE SPACE

WHAT'S on my MIND

"I don't get a hello this morning?" Gene says.

"Sorry. Morning, Gene."

Then I say, "Hi, Nora!" Just in case something has changed over the weekend. She doesn't look up. I sit in the seat behind her and silently unzip the front pocket of my pack. Then I stand and drop my note.

At our lockers, I recite the note to Brooke. "You're sure she has it?" Brooke asks. "She didn't leave it on the bus?" I'm not sure of anything, but there's not much I can do about it.

"Can we talk about something else?" I ask, and shut my locker.

"Wait, don't shut it!" Brooke says. "I have something that will cheer you up."

She reaches into her locker and hands me a rolled-up piece of paper.

I turn my back to the locker so no one else can see. "How did you get this?" I whisper.

Colin's Self-portrait (He is better looking than this, FYI, no offense, Colin!)

"He left it at my house a couple of Fridays ago. He didn't want to take it home. His mother frames all of his self-portraits."

"And you're just giving it to me now?"

"I was going to wait until your birthday."

I roll it up and put it in my locker. "You know, I don't think Mrs. Petty ever gave me mine."

"Today's an F day. Ask her for it."

I am seriously considering it until the actual time comes. Mrs. Petty sets a personal attendance record of nine minutes and thirty-nine seconds, which gives us more time for our new lesson. "Today we are discussing negative space. Who can define the term 'negative space'?"

neg·a·tive space The space in between or around the subject

negative
⁎space⁎
i.e., space around Mrs. Petty

There are teachers who make you want to answer their questions. Mrs. Petty is not one of them. She answers herself. "Negative space is the space between and around things." She sets a vase on the table and we all gather for another demonstration. She takes five minutes to make sure no one is touching each other or the table.

Mrs. Petty begins drawing from the outside edges of her hot-dog paper. We have all gotten the idea after about thirty seconds, but we are in a zombie trance and we cannot move until she finishes her vaahze.

AND ANOTHER THING

Mrs. Petty and I DON'T have in common:
She says VAAHZE, I say VASE.

Do you SEE A VASE or FACES?
(or a VAAHSE or FAAHSES?) I crack. myself. up. Sometimes.

By the time we get back to our seats, we have exactly ten minutes for our drawings. I begin at the outside edges of my hot-dog paper. But when Mrs. Petty announces that we have five minutes left, I draw the vase in the middle of the paper and began scribbling madly to color the rest in.

"Pencils down, everybody!" You can hear the pencils hitting the tables. "Pencil down, Kate!" I let my pencil fall on the paper. "Now, who finished their drawings?"

I was so close, I would have raised my hand if anyone else did. "That's right, nobody, because this is a new process. It takes longer for your brain." She held up Thomas's ("a wonderful beginning"), and Eliza is "on her way." Then she comes to mine. "Do you mind, Kate?" I don't, but my elbows do. They make it hard for her to slide my paper out. "Now, did anybody else do this? This is the way we are used to drawing, by outlining the positive space."

"Mrs. Petty, I was actually outlining the inside edge of the negative space."

NEGATIVE SPACE POSITIVE SPACE

half empty

half full

WHAT'S the DIFF?

"Kate, I'm very pleased you did it this way so the others could understand the difference. You'll have plenty of time to redo it correctly next class."

RATSA and DOUBLE · RAZA

Mrs. Block surveys the class to see how close we are to a consensus. The celebration is four days away.

Columbus Day ~~HHt~~ I
Native American Day ~~HHt~~
Día de la Raza ~~HHt~~
Indigenous People's Day ~~HHt~~
Explorers' Day II
Resistance Day I
Harvest Day I
Italian American Day I

The six of us who voted for Columbus Day are sitting in the back of the room. It looks like we are winning. But now that Mrs. Block has written all the other suggestions on the whiteboard, anybody can see they are all different names for the same thing.

It's impossible not to overhear Brookoberta using her Spanish accent, "Día de la RRRRaza—day of the rrrrace-ah."

"If they take this holiday away," Thomas Bergen-Roosevelt says, "I will protest." Ferdinand, Isabella, Eliza, and Peter agree.

Just then, the mayor of Berkeley, California, walks up and asks to speak with us. "I am proud to say my city held one of the very first Columbus Day celebrations. I am also proud to say we were one of the very first to celebrate Indigenous People's Day. As a leader"—she looks directly at Thomas—"I am here to tell you that you can officially change your mind."

Brookoberta comes over next. "Día de la Roots-a. A day where we celebrate your—our roots. You are Spanish; you celebrate your Spanish-ness. Peter, you are Italian American; you celebrate your Italian-American-ness. You are Creestobal Colon—" She makes a snake hiss and leaves.

co·lon Large intestine, part of the bowel

Colon

ir·ri·ta·ble co·lon Common disorder of the bowel

Irritobal colon

"You know, I think I could celebrate Roots Day," Peter says, and he joins the other side of the room. Thomas, Ferdinand, and Isabella are looking like they could, too, but the five-minute bell rings.

"Okay, kiddos—5B," Mrs. Block catches herself.

"Time to clean up and pack up." She turns the lights off.

LIGHTS OFF = SCHOOL CANDLELIGHT

"Think she'll have an answer?" Brooke asks on our way out to the bus.

"She's not going to give us an answer; we're supposed to be building consensus. Stss-stss?! Did you really have to? You knew what kind of a day I was having," I say.

"I was talking about Nora, not Mrs. B. And I didn't have to, but it was fun. Sorry."

"Never mind," I say. "It's okay. I'll see you tomorrow."

"Gene?" Nora isn't on the bus yet. "Did you find any letters on the bus?"

"Let's see, I have an E-X-I-T. . . . You expecting a love letter?" He smiles.

"She's looking for this," Nora says, dangling the envelope in front of her. I reach for it and she pulls it away.

"Are we talking? Because if we're talking, my dad wants you to come over today. He really wants to show you some pulley system he made for the haunted house."

We're not talking. How original.

Another INVENTION IDEA:
TAKE the GUESSWORK out of
your next silent treatment
with my NEW
SILENT TREATMENT

≡ | ON | OFF |

SIGN

COLON EXPLODES

Ferdinand, Isabella, and Roosevelt deserted on Wednesday.

Brookoberta is impressed. "Implore?! Did you memorize that speech?" she asks before we get to the music room.

"I could almost go for your Roots Day," I say, "but I don't think we'll get Eliza."

We are five minutes late to band and the door is locked. Nora sees us, but we have to knock.

"Take your seats quickly," Mr. Bryant says. Nora has taken the first seat. I sit beside her. I don't say anything the whole time.

I DON'T SAY ANYTHING...

when it's time to play

OR

when Jacob puts his old spitty reed on Nora's seat

When Brooke and I get to Guides, Nora is sitting in the far corner of the cafetorium again. As president of the month, Brooke delegates Nora-duty to Mrs. Hallberg. I am liking the idea of my February short-month presidency better and better all the time.

Brooke reads the announcements, and after we say our promise, she turns the meeting over to Mrs. Staughton. "Girls, I couldn't resist this special Columbus Day activity, which dovetails so nicely with our new concept of 'voyages.' We still have two weeks to pull together the loose ends for our Fall Fun Day. Let's give today's meeting to Columbus. When I say Columbus, what do you think of? Maybe I should say 'who'?"

Elsa, who is not in Mrs. Block's class, says, "The *Niña*, the *Pinta*, and the *Santa María*."

"The *Niña*, the *PintOH*, and the *Santa María*, the three boats that made the epic voyage to America. Today, we are going to create our own epic voyages, using our imaginations and all of our materials. Think about a destination— someplace you've always wanted to go. It can be real or maybe it's someplace that only exists up here." She points to her head.

Mrs. Hallberg gives us each an epic-sized piece of white poster board. "I also have black, in case anyone is thinking about heading into outer space," Mrs. Staughton says, like she is reading my mind.

*Oh yea.
I am thinking
of heading
to outer space...
SO I DON'T HAVE TO
DO THIS PROJECT.*

"If you're having trouble getting started," she says, eyeballing my epically blank white poster board, "perhaps the materials will provide some inspiration!" She takes a silk flower off the table and puts it behind her ear.

my INSPIRATION
Hot glue GUN

flowers
+ fabrics

buttons

pompoms

popsicle
sticks

At 4:40, Mrs. Staughton's alarm goes off. "Ten more minutes, girls! And then we'll each share a few words about our voyages."

I don't have a voyage. I have a hot glue fest.

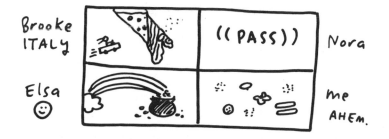

"Mine is actually the voyage itself — all the discoveries you make along the way, which can be more important than the destination," I explain.

"What a wonderful project to end on," Mrs. Staughton says as we form our closing circle.

"I don't think we can fit that in my mom's car," Brooke says when we're in the hall.

"That's okay, I think it'll fit right in here." I put my voyage in the trash. Brooke looks at hers and tosses it in, too.

The next morning there is an envelope on the seat behind Nora.

> I am NOT a project.
> Not yours. Not Brooke's.
> Not your dad's. Projects
> are things that people
> waste their time on and
> end up in the trash.
>
> <u>Not</u> yours,
>   Nora

I lean forward and say "Sorry" loudly. So I am sure she heard it over the bus noise and everything.

I take out a spiral notebook and start writing back.

> Dear Nora,
>   over.   me
> I am <u>sorry</u> you heard Brooke and I
> calling you a project. I agree I would not
> want to be anybody's project, either. But,
> not all projects end up in the trash. I
> save some of them forever. In the begin-
> ning being friends was our moms' idea,
> but I wish you had overheard what I
> was thinking. You weren't a project any
> more. We were friends. I hope you will
>   (friends)
> accept my apology so we can be again.
>   Sincerely,
>   Kate

When I'm done, I fold up the note and put it in my pocket.

YEK, RATSA · A STAR, KEY
(It's a palindrome!)

Specials :
A GYM   We have a Golden Eagle Assembly
B HEALTH   at 10 a.m.
(C LIBRARY)
D COMPUTER
E MUSIC
F ART

Brooke and I each got a school star at the assembly.

On a scale of "deals"

INFINITESIMAL   School   HUGE
                 Star

When Mr. Lovejoy calls Mrs. Petty to the podium to present some art awards, Brooke and I start a game of dots and boxes. "Look up!" Brooke says. (It's not a trick.) My self-portrait is filling the whole screen; my head, for example, is about forty times the size of Mrs. Petty's.

"The *Suburban Times Weekly* has awarded the Gold Key Award for best self-portrait to Katherine Geller." She looks as surprised as I feel.

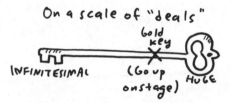

On a scale of "deals"

INFINITESIMAL — Gold Key (Go up onstage) — HUGE

ARRh. The GREAT GO UP on STAGE Dilemma: which way do you face as you exit row...butt in 5B's faces, or hitting backs of people in front?

In class, Mrs. B officially congratulates me and everyone who earned a school star. "In other news," she says, "we reached consensus. Who would like to give the update?" Then she adds, "Let's use our student-identities."

"We came up with the idea of Discovery Day. Each of us will celebrate a discovery," Ronan explains.

"Does that sound okay?" Mrs. Block looks at the others and then at me. I nod.

Nora does not have a note for me on the bus. (Or a hello. Or eye contact.) But I am not going to let it ruin my golden star-key day.

My mom is at the island when I walk in the kitchen door. "What're you doing here?" I say.

"I live here?" She swats the top of my head with a piece of mail. "How 'bout, 'Mom, what a great surprise! So nice to see you!'? Dad's stuck in a meeting, and there was nothing keeping me at the office."

I put the star and the key on the counter. "Gene put my name in for the gold star, and the other one is from the newspaper for my self-portrait."

"Ahh! A judge who knows noses." My mom squeezes me tight.

"What's it for?" Fern asks, reaching for the key.

"Probably an indoor swimming pool with a toy-candy-pet shop," my mom answers. Fern's eyes get super-big. "Everybody in the car! Warm apple dumplings on the way to soccer practice—we're celebrating!"

Let's see.. WHAT COULD THIS KEY BE FOR???

AT PRACTICE...

Sorry.
- Non-soccer Mom

Heh.heh
- A. Dumpling

The next morning, there is an envelope on my bus seat. From Nora, I'm sure. I open it loudly.

> My mother wants to hire us to play duets in the mall VIP shoppers' lounge from 1-3 on Columbus Day. $25 each. She thinks we're friends. If we ever were, please say yes.
> Nora

We watch Nora walk into the building, and then I show Brooke the note. "For twenty-five dollars? I'd do it," Brooke says. "Not that she asked me. Besides, I can't. We're going to the shore."

"It feels weird. It says right there that we're not friends, but it doesn't say anything about maybe being friends again," I say. "We'll have to practice at least once over the weekend. And have you ever heard of the VIP shoppers' lounge?"

"I hate shopping," Brooke says. "You don't have to answer right away. Nora never does."

I put the note in the front pocket of my backpack and I don't think about it again.

"I'm bracing myself for Discovery Day," I say.

Brooke does her best Rigoberta head wrap at her locker and smiles. "It's almost over, Cristobal."

I go last. There were a lot of things I couldn't say: Obviously I, Christopher Columbus, did not discover America.

I, Kate, discovered a lot about Christopher Columbus, and what it feels like to be an outsider, but those weren't things Columbus would say.

"I discovered the trade winds in the Atlantic Ocean, and that discovery has helped sailors ever since," I say. It doesn't seem like much compared to America, so I keep going. "I guess I also discovered that history changes. For almost two hundred years, there were parades in my honor. Now I'm barnacles on a boat bottom."

Mrs. Block smiles. "History is a story, Admiral Colon, and stories have a lot to do with point of view."

"Can we have our snacks as ourselves, please?" I ask. And Mrs. Block nods.

"Did you write to Nora?" Brooke asks on our way out to the bus circle.

"I'm going to tell her I have to talk to my mom first. I don't want to write something and then have to wonder whether she read it . . . again."

I sit behind Nora and talk to the back of her head. "I have to ask my parents," I say. "It isn't a yes or a no."

"Yes, it's not," she mutters, so I know she heard.

V. I. P.

Five minutes after I get home, my mom and Fern walk in the door.

"Mom, Nora's mother wants me and Nora—"

"Nora and me . . ."

"Mom, please! She wants Nora and me to play duets at the mall on Monday. And she'll pay us twenty-five dollars." I show her the note.

"Tricky," my mom says. "Kate, you know you two were friends, whether you agree to play or not. What are you thinking?"

ON the ONE HAND... It's a CHANCE to BE FRIENDS.

ON the OTHER HAND... It FEELS LIKE MRS. KLEIN is PAYING ME to BE NORA'S FRIEND.

ON the THIRD* HAND... It is = $25.

* money-grubbing mutant hand

"I'm not sure about your first hand. The chance to be friends—that part isn't really clear, is it?" my mom says. "And as for your other hand, it sounds like Mrs. Klein already thinks you are friends, and I'm sure she has an entertainment budget, but your feelings are more important than either of those facts, Kate. You should do what feels right.

Doing what feels right $\overset{?}{=}$ Doing what doesn't feel wrong

"I can't imagine being in that mall one second longer than I have to be," Mom says. "I'll give her mom a call."

"I want to talk to Nora after," I say as I hand my mom the phone. "She has to talk to me. I absolutely won't do it if she's not talking to me."

Finally my mom hands me the phone and yells down the hall, "Robin! Adam! Fern! Dinner's ready!"

"I am only doing this if you're talking to me," I say to Nora.

"Of course, Kate. I'm really looking forward to it! See you tomorrow, then!"

Nora's mom drops her off after lunch on Saturday. We go up to my room with the *Easy Duets* book her mom bought. Rocky follows us. Nora is not talking to me, so I talk to Rocky. "Of course, Kate. I'm really looking forward to it!"

"My mother was standing right there," Nora says.

Nora and I choose five duets for a total of ten minutes' playing time.

Easy DUETS MADE HARD
by

(can't count my way out of a)
PAPER BAG PRINCESS
NORA

(((Ah oooooh)))

(Let me take another-)
SOLOIST
ROCKY

"I'm ready to go home now," Nora announces after we play the fifth one for the third time.

"You two were awfully quiet," my mom says as soon as Nora's out the door. "How did it go?"

"Fine, once you accept the fact that she can't keep the beat. I guess playing duets is like talking in a way. And listening."

SHOWTIME

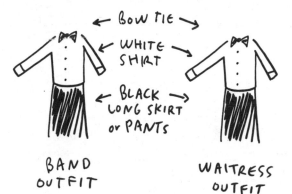

BAND OUTFIT

WAITRESS OUTFIT

I am waiting outside for Nora and Mrs. Klein. My mom says, "You look adorable."

"Adorable, Mom?! In this outfit? All the other bands get to wear pants and short-sleeve shirts," I say.

She laughs as I shuffle down the walk to Mrs. Klein's car.

Mrs. Klein asks a million questions on the ride. I am dreaming of ye olde silent treatment days. "You should have a very nice audience," she says when she finally runs out of questions. "There were about twenty people in the lounge when we left."

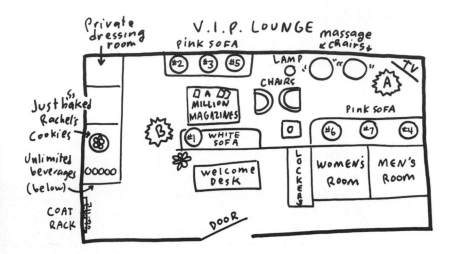

1:00 We begin playing at Location A.

1:03 VIP #6 puts earbuds in.

1:04 VIP #4 requests TV remote and turns TV on.

1:06 We move to Location B.

1:10 VIP #6 leaves.

1:11 VIP #2 asks if we take requests.

1:13 I want to ask VIPs #3 and #5 if they take requests, like BE QUIET!

1:15 The clothes rack of size 2 pants for VIP #5 catches Nora's flute.

It takes all my strength to say to Nora, "You have to get off of me and show me where the nice bathroom is or I may wet my pants." And she does.

Nobody seems to mind—or notice, for that matter— when we take a break.

1:25 We try all the lotion samples in the bathroom.

1:30 We begin playing again at Location B.

1:32 New VIP #8 enters and takes #6's spot.

1:35 VIP #8 inquires about a scent-free VIP club.

1:37 Mrs. Klein gives us each $25, plus $20 for pizza.

"How did the duets go, Champ?" my dad asks at dinner. "That's not blood on your shirt I'm looking at."

"Funny, Dad. It's pizza," I say, and I list all the positives.

How it went: The Sunny side ☺

1. We made $35 each.
2. We had a great laugh.
3. It's over.
4. We got pizza.
5. I think we're friends.

"We'll have to have Nora over more often," my dad says.

"She doesn't want to be anybody's project," I remind him.

"Nora is your friend, not your best friend. She's also a neighbor, and you know her dad's away, plus her mom works a lot. You might think about having her over more often. As a friend. *Not* a project."

There is an envelope sitting next to Nora the next morning. I guess we're back to the silent treatment. Nora shoves the envelope toward the end of the bus seat as I walk by.

Kate
You can sit with me.

She moves her backpack so I can sit down.

 I open the envelope. "It's from my mother," Nora says.

"I actually had fun," I say.

"Yeah," she says while she is reading. Reading makes me carsick, so I just slide down, put my knees up against the seat in front, and pretend to relax.

Brooke acts like it's normal when Nora and I get off the bus together. "How were the duets?" she asks. Nora and I turn to each other and burst out laughing.

V.I.P. Story (Duet/Trio)

ME

The place is ALL pink and gold and this one lady

NORA

So, we start playing. At first, we're

BROOKE

Brooke is laughing by the time VIP #6 puts her earbuds in, and we score a snort when the clothing rack knocks us over.

Nora says "See you" when she heads to her locker.

"See you at lunch," Brooke says. "Hey, why don't you sit with us?"

I think Brooke meant "You should sit with us!" But Nora answers like it's a real question: "I like where I sit." Brooke looks surprised. Nora adds, "Nothing against you."

FUN FUN FUN

At the closing ceremony, Mrs. Staughton takes over. "Fall Fun Day is just a few days away. We are coming to the end of our first voyage. I would like you to close your eyes and think back to where we started six weeks ago.

Six weeks ago, we set out
from the shores of Armpit Lake...

"When I ask you to open them again, I would like each of you to share one thing you have learned along the way."

ONE THING I HAVE LEARNED

what I think:

Mrs. Staughton's fanny pack can't fix everything.

what I say:

I thought I would miss badges but I don't.

Brooke's mother is leaning against her car waiting for us. The leaves are drifting down around her like snow. "I have your bacon costume, Kate!" she says as soon as we're close enough. And she holds it up.

"Hide that!" Brooke says.

"Happy early birthday!" Mrs. Johnson says.

I hug her. "My mom has cupcakes and the banana bread covered." Our moms have an arrangement—Brooke's mom can't cook, and my mom can't sew. I've gotten three excellent costumes out of the deal.

"Brooke's egg still needs a little work. Make sure you try this on before the costume parade on Saturday, just in case."

I try it on the second I get home. "Sizzlin'!" my dad says.

Robin says, "Cute," like it's a new pair of pants or something. She goes back to setting the table.

For example:
~~FR~~
TACO NIGHT
—————

Bowl #1

CHEESE

Bowl #2

TOMATO

Bowl #3

Dad's GROSS
(OOPS. ORGAN
Sorry!) MEAT

"Kate, I'll be glad when your party is over!" My dad has been spending more and more time in the basement and leaving more and more weird stuff all over the house.

"Rob, do you have any advice or anything—it's my first slumber party," I ask.

She taps her fork on the table. "Sleep."

"Seriously?"

"It's your party, and you have to be, you know, 'on,' festive, the next day, too," she says.

"I meant fun things—games and stuff like that," I say.

"We always played Truth or Dare. And somebody's underwear has to end up in the freezer."

My mom walks in. "Kids are still doing that? It used to be the first person who fell asleep. What about sticking somebody's hand in warm water while they're sleeping?"

"It's supposed to make them wet the bed, but it never works," Robin says.

"No shaving cream, hear me, Kate?" Mom says, and walks out again.

"Have you ever played Light as a Feather, Stiff as a Board?" Robin asks. "Maybe we can get Mom and Dad to play after dinner."

mostly FUN DAY

I try very hard to get a good night's sleep before my sleepover.

5:31 a.m. Is it almost time for Fall FunDay? z z z z z	**11:13 a.m.** It's really almost time, Fern!

"Sheesh! Feels more like Summer Fun Day!" Mrs. Staughton says. She is already down to her short sleeves.

The inflatable fun is all set up. Mrs. Hallberg is helping Lily, Elsa, and Faith fill the duck pond over by the jumpy house. Allie and Heather are planting the beanbag toss in front of the shady spot Brooke and I were considering for our bake-sale table. We move our table in front of the main entrance.

MEET Mr. Hallberg
unofficial POD 429 Waterboy

Remember to hydrate!

Gives unofficial reminders every 10 secs.
(I'll try not to bore you with them.)

Eliza and Nora put their face-painting table right next to us.

Fern and Mom are the first Fall Fun Day guests to arrive. My mom takes pictures with her real camera, and Fern runs straight to the face-painting table. "Balloons, please," she says.

"Oh, phew. Balloons are easy," Nora says.

"Don't you want a . . . ?" Brooke starts to say, leafing through their design book. Nora glares at her.

Nora paints three balloons and holds the mirror up. "More, please," Fern says.

Nora paints three more on the other cheek and shows Fern. "More, please." Nora looks at me, and I shrug. Nora paints three balloons on Fern's forehead and gets another "More, please."

My mom leans in. "Nine is enough, Fern-o. I think I see your friend Jack in line at the duck pond—why don't we give that a try?"

Ten minutes later, Fern drops a handful of duck-pond prizes— plastic bugs, stickers, and a ring—on the bake-sale table. "I wanted to win a big prize," Fern says.

"Let's give everybody else a chance. How about the jumpy house?" my mom says. "Fern was afraid to go while Mrs. Staughton was in there cooling off."

"Oh, snap!" Nora says. "How about a witch instead of a frog?" Her five-year-old ~~customer~~ victim nods. Nora proceeds to paint his whole face.

His mother asks, "Does this come off with soap and water?"

Nora looks at Eliza. Eliza says, "I think so. Definitely."

Nora comes over to ask me if we can trade places. "You're more of an artist."

"I'm actually not very good at face painting," I tell her.

"Really?"

"You don't have to look so shocked, Nora," I say.

Reasons why I'm NOT good at face-painting:

1. There is no brush control.
2. Bad flashback☻ (Time I used Sharpies)
3. See #1.

Brooke offers to ask her mother, and Mrs. Johnson takes over face painting. Meanwhile, my mom is talking to Nora's mom over by the duck pond. Fern is in line again. She does not win the big prize. She goes for another and its tail bobs just out of reach.

The next kid in line follows Fern into the "pond," then four more after him. They are all turning and tossing ducks until there are practically none left in the pond.

Mrs. Staughton blows her whistle. "This is a DUCK POND, not a swimming pool." Except everyone can see the opposite is true.

Mr. Hallberg sticks his hand in the pool. "Nice and cool in there."

I ask Mrs. Staughton to blow her whistle again so we can begin our first cupcake walk.

"When the music starts, you all walk in a circle around the plates, like musical chairs. And when the music stops, you stop. If you're standing closest to plate number one, you get to pick your cupcake first. Number two, second . . ." Brooke holds up the box of prize cupcakes. "Everybody ready?" I turn on the music and count to forty-seven.

"Next time, don't mention musical chairs," Brooke says.

The parents help the kids out of their cupcake pants into the duck-pond-wading-pool. There are two more incident-free cupcake walks, and then Mrs. Staughton blows her whistle again. It is time for the costume parade.

Mr. Hallberg herds everybody over to the pool-pond.

"For those of you who don't know me, I am Marian Staughton, Pod 429's new leader. On behalf of Pod 429, thank you all for coming to our Fall Fun Day. A little history—Fall Fun Day was actually started in honor of another F-word. Can anybody guess?"

"Our *founder,* Helen Seidlar. Now, as a new leader, I decided I would like to begin a new tradition today. I have a small award I would like to present to the Guide who embodies Dr. Seidlar's spirit—a woman who believed that the two most important things you can do in this life are to stand up for yourself and to stand up for others. Kate Geller, will you please come forward?"

"I am pinning this on upside down because, in the inspirational words of Dr. Seidlar, 'A rainbow upside down is a smile right side up.'"

I admit, I like Mrs. Staughton better now. She actually gave me an award for disagreeing with her. Most grown-ups find that annoying.

"Let the parade begin!" Mrs. Staughton says, too loudly again, into the microphone. But that is when a large piece of toast falls down.

"Nora fainted!" Brooke says, kneeling down beside her. Mrs. Klein makes her way over. Mr. Hallberg follows her with a bottle of water.

Mrs. Staughton says, "Don't crowd her!" as she is rummaging through her fanny pack. "Smelling salts, coming through!" Everyone moves out of the smelling salts' way.

DR. SEIDLAR

"I'm fine," Nora says, and stands up by herself.

"I'm going to take her home," Mrs. Klein says to Mrs. Staughton.

"But she's still coming to my birthday party, right?" blurts the bacon.

"Kate, her mother will sort this out." My mom puts her arm around me.

"I'll let you know how she's doing," Mrs. Klein says.

"Bacon, eggs, and toast! Very clever!" Mr. Hallberg says.

I look at Brooke in her egg costume and say, "Wait, how did Nora know what we were going to be?"

MEIN HAUS IS HAUNTED

Everyone arrives for my party at once. I have to admit, it is pretty perfect, with the car headlights shining behind them through the fog and mist.

Once the jumble of bags (gift, overnight, and sleeping) gets organized, Mom and Robin serve the pizza. My dad brings Fern down in her pajamas, and she climbs into Hui Zong's lap.

"Did you hear from Nora?" Eliza asks. "Is she coming?"

"Her mom is going to bring her over in the morning," my mom answers. Eliza and Brooke groan.

"Evening, girls! When you're ready, I'd like to show you your accommodations."

Our "Innkeeper"

WARNING: Object may be scarier than it appears. APOLOGY: I am not good at scary drawing.

He opens the basement door, and the nine of us huddle on the top three stairs. "Watch your step. I've been meaning to fix these." He shines his flashlight down on a rat. Lily screams. "Dead as a dormouse," my dad says, and picks it up. "Hold this, will you?" Elsa refuses, so he stuffs the rat in his flannel shirt pocket.

"Careful now," Dad says at the bottom of the stairs. He shines his light on the corner of the basement. "That bed there is very comfortable. Someone like to try it?" Faith starts laughing and goes over. "Give it a sit!" A skeleton's arm shoots out from under the blanket and Faith jumps. Allie screams. "Sorry, sir," he apologizes to the arm. "I forgot the gentleman requested a late checkout."

246

My dad shines the flashlight straight ahead. "Guest privileges—we just ask that you leave everything as you found it."

Our "KITCHEN"

BLOOD

PEEK at the "PANTRY"
miscellaneous gross junk

pickled brains

more sick stuff

EYEBALLS

ICE-COLD peeled grapes

BEATING HEART

squirts blood

INTESTINE.
TAPEWORM SALAD

spaghetti.
fettucine

↑ ALL·U·
FREE CAN.
~ EAT

"NIBBLIES"

"Well, you get the idea. You girls have the run of the place. Let's get your bags and make you comfortable—" There is a bloodcurdling scream, followed by eight more bloodcurdling screams.

"Dad, someone's on the floor!" I say.

"Sorry, watch your step," he says.

"I'm serious, it's not funny. Turn the lights on!"

I'm so happy to see Nora, I hug her, even with that gross newspaper stuck on her.

SLUMBER PARTY ≠ SLEEP

My dad clears off the basement floor for our sleeping bags.

"Cake is served!" Mom calls.

oh, yum!

BLOODY EYEBALL CAKE

Dad comes into the kitchen, all showered and shaved, as we are finishing our cake. Everyone starts clapping.

"Did I miss something?" He winks.

CRINGE-O-METER

I ♥ MY DAD!

After cake, we watch *Beetlejuice* and have popcorn. Nora falls asleep during the movie. Brooke goes to get her underwear. "We shouldn't," I say. "This could make her swear off birthday parties forever." I have to wake Nora up to go downstairs to sleep.

~~light~~ TICKLY as a feather

I am the second one up the next morning. My dad is reading the paper at the kitchen table. "You get any sleep, Champ?"

"Mm," I say.

"How do silver-dollar pancakes sound for breakfast?" I give him a thumbs-up. By the time the batter is ready, we're all awake (except Robin).

After breakfast, everybody packs up. Mrs. Staughton is the last parent to pick up. "Adam, word is this was the best slumber party ever! I don't know how you're going to top it."

"I've got a whole year to work on it," he says, smiling the innkeeper's smile.

SAYONARA SINGLE DIGITS

For an untraditional family, we sure have a lot of BIRTHDAY TRADITIONS

BREAKFAST

"<u>Good</u> morning, Gene!" I say when I get on the bus, because it is extra-good.

"Not so fast, young— I should say ol' lady!" He turns and hands me a birthday pencil with a birthday stick of gum. "Happy birthday, Kate!"

"Is your birthday almost over?" Nora says when I sit down beside her. "I get to stay home on mine." I can't imagine staying home and missing Mr. Lovejoy announcing my birthday on the loudspeaker or everybody singing at morning meeting. "What did you get from your parents?"

"I don't know yet," I say. She opens her book and reads the rest of the way to school.

Brooke, Nora, and I walk into school together, as usual. Mr. "Killjoy" shakes my hand. "Happy birthday, my friend!"

Mrs. Block smiles when I walk in. "Happy birthday, Kate! You know, I loved being ten."

It sounds like something Robin would say.

Mrs. Block hands everybody a star on their way in from my birthday recess. They have to write a birthday wish and pass them in.

Nice 3RD-grade tradition

FLASH-BACK!

Then Mrs. Sanelli comes down to take us to library. She and Mrs. Block keep looking over at me as they're talking. I smile a nice birthday smile back.

As I walk by the checkout desk, Mrs. Wright wishes me a happy birthday and hands me a birthday bookmark. I pivot and head for my book stash at the end of Biography Row.

(Mrs. SANELLI'S REEBARKS)

"This?" There were so many this-es.

"I am aware it's your birthday today. Mrs. Block and I had a conversation. I don't want to punish you on your birthday, but THIS has to stop. Do you understand me?" I nod. "TODAY."

I stack the books and stand up. "Do NOT, I repeat, do NOT consider reshelving those yourself. You may take them up to the front and Mrs. Wright will place them on the cart. No borrowing privileges today."

"Oh well," Brooke says when we're back in the Book Nook. "Takes the pressure off being perfect for another year."

"How's the birthday so far?" Gene asks at the end of the day.

"Mostly good," I say. "Gene, when's your birthday, anyway?"

"December twenty-fifth," he says.

"You must get gypped."

"I'm doing all right, doing ALL right," he says. When he smiles, the back of his head wrinkles.

The BACK of GENE's head SMILES

OK, I added eyes, but still.

Nora is not doing all right.

"Sorry my birthday is so annoying," I say as I sit down.

"Everything's annoying, but I'm trying not to annoy you on your birthday," she says.

"It's not me that's annoying, just my birthday, right?"

"Okay, that's annoying," she says.

I'm quiet for a while. Then I say, "But you're still coming trick-or-treating?" She nods. We're quiet the rest of the way.

ELEVEN CANDLES

Grammalolo comes to my birthday dinner, even though she does not care for stuffed peppers or lemon desserts. "I think it's her way of letting you know she thinks you're extra-special, Champ," my dad says. My mother sighs and shakes her head.

Grammalolo shoves a big present in front of me after the table is cleared. "It was your mother's," she says. Grammalolo has a habit of wrapping up my mother's old things for our birthdays. Robin got a lot of the best stuff because Grammalolo wasn't sure she was going to have any more grandchildren.

"Oh, Mom," my mother says. "I can't believe you saved that!" It's her favorite sweatshirt from when she was ten. I try for a second to imagine her in it.

"Can I give her these now?" Grammalolo asks.

"Hold on a second—your mother and I have this for you," my dad says.

Good for
* TWO *
pierced ears!

(no cash value)

HAPPY 10th!

I hope you
love Harry
Potter

"and riding
your bike"

LOVE,
Mom + Dad

"All right, Lois," Dad says to Grammalolo. "Now it's your turn."

She hands me a small unwrapped box. "These were mine." I lift the top. It snaps back and rests on its hinges. "They were my very first pair. I got them when I was ten."

(sparkly blue
in middle)

TRUE!! GMALOLO
was 10 once.

I go over and hug her. Fern hands me an envelope. "They're Rocky's whiskers," she says before I have a chance to open it.

"Wow, Fernie. Where'd you find them?"

"Find them . . . yes . . ." My mother makes a snipping motion. "Fern, come help me get the pie!"

"Shhh," Fern says, and points at me.

I blow out all eleven candles and wish the same wish I always wish that hasn't come true. (And I can't tell you, or it never will.)

Then my dad starts the last of our birthday traditions: "Ten things we love about Kate!"

"Adam, I will NOT let you do this for my birthday this year," Grammalolo says. "We'll be here all night."

Ten actually go by fast. My mom writes them all down and puts them in my birthday book. Fifty-five in all, now.

ROBIN "made" me a REAL (magic 8 Ball with sticker)

KATEBALL !!!

WRAP-UP

"Your friend's in a much better mood," Gene says when I get on the bus the next morning.

Nora asks what I got for my birthday. When I tell her, she says, "Are you going to get them done at the mall?"

OPPOSITE of the SILENT TREATMENT

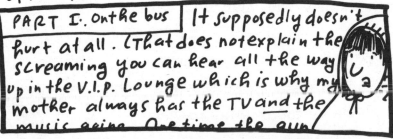

PART I. On the bus | It supposedly doesn't hurt at all. (That does not explain the screaming you can hear all the way up in the V.I.P. Lounge which is why my mother always has the TV and the music going. One time the gun

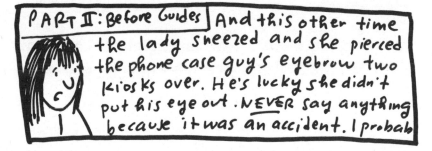

PART II: Before Guides | And this other time the lady sneezed and she pierced the phone case guy's eyebrow two kiosks over. He's lucky she didn't put his eye out. NEVER say anything because it was an accident. I probab

Mrs. Staughton confers with Brooke, then announces that we will be switching pod presidents a week early since November is an extra-short meeting month. Allie is now technically the president, but

Mrs. Staughton sits her down. "You girls all did a wonderful job on Saturday. Now we need to shift gears and start to think about our Thanksgiving baskets for the elderly. And, of course, November is the month we hold our annual Harvest Food Drive with the Boy Scouts."

"Except this year"—Allie pounds her presidential fist on the table—"this year, we'll win!"

"Win?" Mrs. Staughton says. "Girls, we're all winners when we collect food. And other nonperishable items."

"It's a contest, Mom," Heather explains. "Last year, the Boy Scouts won the overnight to Luau Keys."

"That place gave my sister a bad rash," Nora says.

"I wasn't aware there were prizes," Mrs. Staughton says.

Mrs. Hallberg steps in. "Allie, why don't you get our Halloween safety game going?"

BIRTHDAY WISH DO-OVER: No stupid games in February! (Just kidding. I wouldn't tell you a real wish.)

On Halloween night, my mom actually makes us wear our Guide Glow Sticks.

"I'm so glad Nora decided to join you," Mom says.

EVERYBODY LOVES GLOWING

Nuclear BACON & Irradiated EGGS

Mrs. Klein drives up. We're cracking up (no egg pun intended) watching Nora get out of the backseat in her costume. "Girls, help her out!" my mom says.

We run over. Brooke grabs Nora's right hand, and as soon as she has cleared the door, I grab her left. Nora and Brooke can't walk side by side without knocking each other, so I try to stay in the middle.

I catch up. My mom snaps a picture.

We are a threesome. A strange threesome. But we've come a long way.

 In my next GREAT book...

#1 Pod 429 takes on Pack 22. The Farley's Fourth Harvest Food Drive turns into a showdown for the:

 GRAND PRIZE OVERNIGHT at Luau Keys WATERPARK HOTEL

 Rash City!

Who will win?
Let's ask.

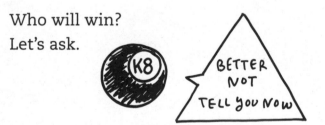 K8 — BETTER NOT TELL YOU NOW

#2 Someone will have a *moving* experience.

 Is it KATE?

 MY REPLY IS NO

#3 Mrs. Staughton will astonish.   *The* FANNY PACK FREAK SHOW!

#4 My dad will bring out his best jokes yet.

   Will they be funny?

FUNNY! (According to an eight ball.)

YES

And don't miss . . .   ABC* GUM

*Already-Been-Chewed

FAKE ~~Flower~~ Fingernails!

ACKNOWLEDGMENTS

Kate owes her greatness in part to the exceptional editing and encouragement of Phoebe Yeh, the art direction of Ken Crossland, the editorial assistance of Rachel Weinick, and the dedication of the rest of the team at Crown Books for Young Readers. I would also like to thank my BAF Edite Kroll, my early readers and guest calligraphers (Brooke James, Kathy McCullough, Audrey Swartz, Kerry Oblak, Aurora Becker, Bella Cotter, and Jessica MacLeish), and the James and Butka families, who provided *Kate* and me with writerly retreats.

↳ Best Agent Forever

ABOUT the AUTHOR-ILLUSTRATOR

 Suzy Becker is best known for her international bestseller *All I Need to Know I Learned from My Cat*. She is the author-illustrator of three other books for kids, one book for babies, and four books for grown-ups. *Kate the Great* is her first illustrated novel. Suzy has also had other jobs: lemonade-stand owner (age seven), greeting-card company mogul (not the ski kind), and one of the cofounders of the Francis W. Parker Charter Essential School. She and her family live in central Massachusetts.

Humorous

Radiant smile

Takes → chances

Nice, caring, good friend

Freckles · · · · · · ·

Can make a 3-leaf clover with tongue

musical

Good at stories

Can say ABC alphabet in < 5 seconds

sensitive

Flexible!

Shares GUM Cooperative

curious

moo*

*Translation: Animal person

Great cook

will always play games

Loves boats

Reprinted with my permission from: